The Prepper
Part One: The Collapse

By Karl A.D. Brown

D1637213

Cover Art: Cover Design by

www.ebooklaunch.com

This novel is dedicated to my wife
and daughter lots of love, K.

Table of Contents

Prologue:

Alfred Aimes stepped out into a clearing on his heavily wooded land with his hands up. There was a short rotund woman, with scraggly black hair, in the clearing. She was maybe about 30, but she was so covered in filth that it was hard for him to be sure. Her face was horribly disfigured. One eye was fused shut and it seemed as if half her face had melted into itself. He had heard of the Syracuse Nuke Survivors but he had never met one to date. He figured that this woman may have drifted down from that irradiated city, or the surrounding area. Many people had survived the initial nuclear terrorist attack on Syracuse but they were basically walking corpses. This one was on his land and he wanted to know why. The fact that she was fat in these lean times further alarmed him, but he kept his face neutral. He put on a disarming grin and began his act.

"My name's Alfred. I hunt in these woods all the time. Is this your land?" he asked keeping his voice apologetic. He intended to see what her answer was going to be and what her intentions were. "I didn't mean to trespass," he continued. Alfi wore camo; his brown hair carefully cropped short giving him a military air. He carried no apparent weapons though, so the woman smiled and relaxed a bit. She had a large machete in her right hand. She seemed to take courage from the fact that she was armed and he was not.

"Get down on the ground put your hands behind your back." She said though ruined lips in her nasally, phlegmy voice as she advanced with the weapon. Just then another person materialized out of the woods and came towards them. It was a man, tall and thin. His skin was just as dirty as the woman and his eyes were a bit insane. "You do what you are told now." He had a small revolver and he waved it at Alfred when he spoke.

"Well I don't want any trouble. I just wanted to know if you owned this land, and if you would allow me to hunt here, I would share anything I harvested with you and your family of course."

"You heard the lady, get down and put your hands behind your back." Alfred got on his knees and before he lay on the ground he realized that the man seemed to be salivating. "So what are you going to do with me?" The man got down and began to unspool a piece of rope from his pants pocket. "Well you are food." He said simply.

"Say that again. I didn't hear it right."

"I said you are food! Food! Food!" The woman joined in she had a crazy grin on her horribly destroyed face. Her teeth were blackened and Alfred realized that he could smell their body odor which was like being next to a rotting corpse. The man then raised his gun, and aiming for Alfred's head he was about to bring the pistol down when there was a single sharp crack of a rifle. The man fell face down on top of Alfred with a hole in the side of his head. The woman snarled and turned to run when another report came from the other side of the clearing. She ran a few steps then fell over; a hole had blossomed in the center of her chest.

Alfred rolled the body off and stood up. Two women, his daughter and wife, materialized out of the woods from opposite sides of the clearing. The younger woman was still in her early teens. She like her mother was wearing camo. She had brown hair like her father and a serious demeanor. Alfred's wife was in her early forties, slender, and her red hair was wrapped into a tight bun under her brown baseball cap. They both carried Ruger M77 Hawkeye Magnum Hunter rifles.

"It was a good thing we saw them before they could sneak up on us," his wife said with a low hard voice.

"Yes it was good that we were able to figure out what their intentions were before they could act. It won't be so clear cut all the time." Alfred picked up the man's gun, an old .22 revolver, checked the cylinder, found there were four rounds in it. He placed the gun in his pocket.

"So what do we do with them now Dad?"

He thought about it for a second before saying, "I think we should drag them over to the Walker's Farm and leave them there." It was a good forty minute walk to the destroyed farm that was on the edge of their property but Alfred decided that he felt a whole lot better with fewer bodies on his land. They linked the bodies together hands to feet and while they worked on dragging them to what would be their final resting place, Alfred could not help wondering how he and his family had come to this. How had America come to this? And while they dragged the bodies of the two people they had just killed, his mind slipped back into the past. 'Never in our wildest dreams did we ever think civilization as we knew it would crumble like this.'

Chapter One: Waking Up

"Few men have virtue to withstand the highest bidder."
George Washington.
*"A government ought to contain in itself every power
requisite to the full accomplishment of the objects
committed to its care, and to the complete execution of
the trusts for which it is responsible, free from every
other control but a regard to the public good and to the
sense of the people."* Alexander Hamilton.
*"The Constitution which at any time exists, 'till changed
by an explicit and authentic act of the whole People is
sacredly obligatory upon all."* George Washington.

Sometime in the near future:

***Alfred Aimes, called Alfi by his
friends, sat on his couch one long hot
evening after work.*** His two children Candice
aged eight, and Robert aged eleven at the time, played
in the living room. They had finished their homework
and still had just over an hour to go before bed. They
were making the most of it. The family had eaten dinner
and Alfred's wife Samantha was now taking a shower.
She would be in there awhile, Alfi knew. It was her way
of unwinding from the day. He was watching an old
movie on the FX channel *Fun with Dick and Jane,* and
laughing a mile a minute. It felt good to laugh. He was a
middle management man like Carrey in the movie, just

without the BMW and the six hundred thousand dollar house. He was a man of more modest means.

The family owned a nice and well-maintained three bedroom house on the outskirts of Binghamton, NY. It was located on an acre of land. They had two cars, a virtual necessity in upstate New York, in a family in which both parents worked. Alfi and Samantha had a quiet middle class lifestyle that some would envy. He was really just like any hard working man in his early forties.

A family man, mortgaged up to the hilt and still trying to pay off the student loan he had acquired in college. He laughed at Carrey's and Tea Leoni's antics and warmed to the actors as he realized that their story, tongue in cheek as it was, was the story of the middle class. The middle class that had grown up believing that if you worked hard and were loyal to your employer, you would be taken care of and the hard work would be rewarded with upward financial mobility.

Then as Alfi watched the fictitious family slide into financial ruin, he felt a chill and a shortening of breath. The smile slowly faded from his face. The whole story of how the little guy was screwed over by the fat cat CEO really hit home. The way the fat cat got away scott free and was able to maintain his lifestyle while the company workers were left holding the bag was how it was in the real world as well. What do we call the fat cats these days he wondered: 'Ahh yes the fabled *one percent*.' A term coined during an election long ago, he couldn't quite remember which.

He frowned as he thought it over. There was a grim hypocrisy to it all. This on*e percent* was the place where most aspired to, but hated while they were not in the club. It was the status which once achieved, was protected at all costs, America's real ruling elite. It was the class to which almost all of the current politicians belonged. The way Alfi figured it the fat cats conned the middle class and the poor. They lulled them with speeches and references to the Constitution and individualism while they lined their pockets, driving the country to ruin. They were anything but individualists. They depended on others for their vast power, whether it was to elect them into office or get them into their positions of leadership. Most CEO's were really good schmoozers. Once in they would greedily line their own pockets, most of the times illegally, finding ways and loopholes to circumvent the laws. Then they would pontificate about the self-made man or woman and smile their fake smiles. When the character in the film said he hoped they got what they deserved, he agreed whole heartedly with the sentiment.

His mind now vacillated, and he began think about how much money he and Samantha had lost from their retirement funds when the stock market tanked again a few years ago. He remembered how she had been laid off, and how much of a panic it caused. They had recovered well; Sam had gone back to school and had finished her nursing degree. She was once again gainfully employed. He had gotten lucky; the city of Binghamton had fought tooth and nail to keep the yogurt factory in the town. It was an employer of thousands of jobs and it would have been a disaster if they had been forced to close. It was a good thing they made damn good Greek style yogurt that people just seemed to crave.

The movie unsettled him though, because it made him begin to wonder about the family's finances. They had tried diversifying their portfolios but somehow he was still ill at ease. The country still had not recovered from the most recent recession. As a good Independent he had gone to the polls whole-heartedly to give all the Presidents from Obama to the present Commander in Chief a shot. He had voted Democratic or Republican based on the candidate's vision for the economy. Hell, in one election he had even voted Libertarian. But the current President much like his predecessors was not able to fully grapple with the scope of the problems, and things were still in a state of flux.

Unemployment continued to be high and the country's debt was still spiraling out of control. A lot of the big cities had gone bankrupt like Detroit. He like a lot of Americans had the unsettling feeling that they were not being told the entire truth, and it left him very uneasy. A sigh escaped him. He was no longer laughing anymore. He heard the shower snap off and knew that Sam would be joining him soon. They were into their routine; the kids would soon go up to bed and they would watch something short on the TV, before retiring soon thereafter themselves.

When Samantha sat down he put his arms around her and said softly as she snuggled up to him: "We always seem to be coming back to the same discussion every few months. Money, money, money! Will our jobs be safe? Will we have enough for our retirement? With all the things seemingly constantly going wrong, it all just feels wrong to me, like we are missing something important." Samantha turned and looked at him. He could smell her freshly shampooed hair. "Well we have done all we can, as most people have to be recession proof. Our retirement money is not tied up in pension programs but individual 401K's and mutual fund accounts. We are certainly not planning on relying on

Social Security or Medicaid. Chances are they won't be around when we retire anyway."

"True, true but..." he sighed.

"I just want to watch the TV, no more bad news tonight okay."

"Okay." He smiled and kissed her hair. His mind continued to turn over though. There must be a way he could find out more about what was going on with the country's finances. He resolved to look into the matter and for a while that's where he left it.

*

He did look into it. He asked an accountant friend of his, Patrick Finnegan, to explain to him just how much the country was in debt. His friend, a tall, pale, wiry man leaned across his desk pushed his glasses up his nose and said: "Well we are in debt up to about 22 trillion dollars."

"So it has gone up since 2014."

"Ohh yes, it's a miracle that we are all still here," came the ironic reply.

A few months after that conversation a few things began to blip on his consciousness. A lot of the big bank CEOs and CFOs began to quit, or were fired from their jobs. Big banks, ones that seemed to prop the world up on their shoulders began to be implicated in all sorts of illegal insider trading fraud schemes. Then there were certain large privately owned corporations that went public and after a lot of hype, their stocks underperformed, actually trading at a loss, but not before their CEOs pocketed large quantities of the dough themselves, becoming even more impossibly wealthy.

But then the thing from which neither he nor the world could turn away from occurred. In Europe the tactic of providing a stimulus plan to struggling countries began to fail. As far as he could make out it seemed that the stimulus would have worked if the countries also adopted stringent austerity measures. But in a world high on greed and narcissism, this was not possible. They continued with their out of control spending to support an unsustainable lifestyle for their citizens. This led to more hyperinflation. Years ago in Greece, which was one of the first to go under; there had been a brief period of stability, even growth. Everyone thought or was led to believe that everything was going to be okay. This was proved false when a couple of years after the bailout they went under. It was a carbon copy of the first scare in which there was a run on the banks, food shortages, and a massive failure of the country's infrastructure. This led to martial law being imposed in the country, which prevented what would have been a complete shattering of the country's social order.

The shocking thing to Alfi was that no one seemed to learn anything from the Greek tragedy, and soon other countries followed. Every eight months or so, a new European country would seem to fall into the headlines as they struggled to stay afloat. Alfi then began to wonder how this would affect the US. He began to do more research online and realized that leading economists and authors had been predicting this very same scenario for years.

He wondered how he could have missed all the signs. How could he not have seen the impending danger this all represented to himself and his family more clearly. He wondered how he would broach the subject with his wife Samantha who was in all respects a very well-grounded woman. This would be just a bit

much, he figured, and he began to camouflage his concern as just a passing interest. He resolved to keep it to himself for now. The big question facing him was what to do about it. Okay it seemed that the world economy was teetering. But there were a lot of really smart people in the world out there, who could help to fix the mess, right? Surely there must be?
*

It was in this uneasy frame of mind that he began looking at the family's finances in a lot more detail and realized that they could be in a lot of trouble as most of their money was tied up in the banks, their retirement funds, their modest savings, everything. The more he researched it the more it appeared to him that this was not as sound a business practice as he had thought. Alfi himself never really even saw his pay, as it was directly deposited into their checking account, and he used his debit card and credit card now more than he used cash. This was a fact that his father frowned upon. His father believed that using cash made people more conscious of their spending habits. He realized that if the banks failed they would be left with little or no cash. A bad scenario if they needed to buy food, or other things. So he ran the idea by Sam to have on hand a rainy day Quick Cash Fund. He resolved to keep at least three grand in cash in the house.

He did ask Patrick about keeping all their money in the banks and if that might not be a good idea. "Well," Pat said, "No one trusts the banks these days. Years ago, do you remember the Cyprus issue?" Alfred shook his head in the negative. "Well most people won't really. What happened in Cyprus blipped in the main stream media and was gone. Well long story short, when their economy tanked the government seized the banks, and the account holders' savings were frozen. They came to a deal which was to take a certain percentage of the account holders' cash to pay down the national debt. This made everyone sit up and take notice, because it had set the precedent for what most countries would do if they found themselves in the same predicament."

"I tell all my clients and you because you are a friend. Spread your money out and diversify as much as possible. Heck it might not be a bad idea to change some of your cash assets into gold or silver, and keep it at home."

*

He then began looking at other deficiencies. Years ago there was a series of massive floods in the Binghamton area. They lived outside of the city in the hills so they were not affected as badly as the people in town were. They were without power for a few hours, and there was some minor damage to the factory and the hospital where Sam worked, but that was all really. They had gotten by with a cooler for the stuff in their freezer, and some candles. It had been for his family a minor inconvenience, but he knew they were lucky. A lot of people, and business owners in the city and surrounding areas had lost everything.

He had thought then about buying a generator, but then pushed the idea away. His rationale had been that it was too expensive and he trusted the power company to restore power quickly if there was an outage. Now looking at the news coming out of the countries in the middle of their economic meltdowns he began to realize that his family was not as prepared for an emergency as they should have been. A couple words from the T.S. Elliot poem, *The Love Song of J. Alfred*

Prufrock flashed through his thoughts. He realized that he was '*Like a patient etherized upon a table'*. He had been in a state of social ignorance and sleep.

Alfi found himself then really looking at his life in a new way. He felt like he had been one of those animals that would get fawned over and fattened up on a farm, not out of love but just so they could be easily led to the slaughter house. He then realized that maybe he had been too reliant on the government, the country's infrastructure, and the good will of his fellow man to take care of him and his family. If there really was a problem, he mused, the only people who could take care of his family, was his family.

He began to go online and really read about preparing for a breakdown of the social order and the country's infrastructure. What he found came as quite a shock. There had been people out there who had been preparing for such scenarios for years. They called themselves preppers. He then went online to Amazon and found a few books on the subject. As far as he was concerned he only wanted to learn about the basics that could get his family through six months if there was no help available. Because as much as he figured there might be a bad time coming, he couldn't see it persisting for more than three to four months before the government reasserted itself, reestablishing social order. He told himself that he was going to be practical. He asked himself then, 'What would my family need to be okay for a while if the brown stuff was to hit the fan for a few months?' It was then he realized that he was indeed very unprepared, and he may not have a lot of time to do anything about it.
*

This thought initially filled him with panic. His mind then flashed back to all the Y2K nut jobs who thought the grid was going to go down. 'Am I like them? Am I just another overwhelmed citizen who has begun to see threats where there are none? Have I been reading too much of this crap? Am I losing my sense of optimism, because of underlying issues in my life?' After really examining himself, the answers all came back no. His concerns were not unreasonable in his view. He would then have to act accordingly.

So where to start? Well what were the major categories? Water, food, shelter, power, communication, health, and protection. He would need somewhere to store all the things his family would need. He had a large detached garage, which ran parallel to his house, and a shed in the backyard. There was also the basement. He decided that a major house cleaning was in order. Get rid of the things he didn't need, keep the essentials, and then use the available space for his prepping needs. He realized that it would take him a week or maybe more to get it all done, but he was resolved in his mind to get the space he needed.

Alfi began with the garage, and then went onto the shed, then the basement. He worked every day after work for two weeks. His wife was amazed at his new-found interest in order and cleanliness, and she welcomed it with open arms. He tried to think strategically. He kept a small tool cache in the garage, but after really looking at his tools he realized that he needed some more essential items, and high on his list was a buzz saw. He also inventoried his tools and made a list of anything he was missing. That weekend he went to Lowes and filled his list. It was amazing what this small step did for his morale, and though it wasn't much it was a step in the right direction.

He began reading that years ago the National Geographic Channel had run a show called "*Doomsday Preppers*", so he ordered the first season on DVD and what he saw not only appalled him but inspired him as well. For while some of the '*preppers*' were over the top, there were a few who he thought had some good ideas. The more he checked around the internet the more he realized that it seemed that most preppers had found the show disturbing because of the way it showcased their way of life. Most of the prepping and preppers portrayed in the show made the lifestyle seem almost like a borderline mental disease, just a bunch of neurotic, paranoid people who believed that the world was going to end. To him and many others, instead of making people understand that being prepared was a good thing, it made the preppers seem like sad delusional people who put not only themselves and their families at risk with their prepping, but also the greater society as well.

Alfi then realized that there seemed to be two types of preppers. There were those who were open about their beliefs and those who kept it all to themselves. He decided that he was going to be in the latter category. To him it didn't seem to be a good idea to let anyone know what he was doing. He then did a mental calculation from the time he realized that something wasn't quite right to the present and he realized that it was coming up on eighteen months. His awakening, he realized, was very gradual. He recognized that despite his hardening resolve, subconsciously he had kept hoping for better news on the economy, which was not forthcoming.

He realized that he was still hoping that the news on the economy would get better. What Alfi did not understand was that he was so focused on one thing he was missing the bigger picture of what was going on in the world. He had just grabbed hold of one small corner of the tapestry which was now unraveling. He was however correct in his resolve to at least prepare for the eventuality of a societal breakdown. His mind kept coming back to the fact that he had a wife and two kids to keep safe if there was ever a problem. He went onto his porch and looked up and down Pine Road. Living on the outskirts of the city, out here was really farm country, with farmers owning most of the land. He had neighbors but they were nicely spaced out along the road. Each house had considerable privacy. As he inhaled the crisp night air he could just make out the Parsons' house lights, and he wondered about his neighbors and what would become of them. Along with those thoughts also came some unsettling questions that he was not ready to ask himself.

*

Samantha came out and slipped her arm around him. She could tell that he was worried, and she knew her husband enough to know that he was keeping something from her. She had her suspicions, and one day would confront him about it. But she decided that the time was not now. She just wanted to enjoy the evening. The children were in bed, and she just wanted to feel the closeness of him. He then turned to her and said, "Tomorrow I think I will look into getting us some personal protection." This made her alarmed. Personal protection meant guns, and as a New York City girl who had come to the countryside to live she was not comfortable with the idea of having firearms in the house, especially with the children around. She shifted away from him. "I really don't think that's a good idea Alfi. Guns are dangerous. We have two very inquisitive children; they could get a hold of one of them and have an accident."

"Don't worry about it. They will have locks and I will be buying a safe to store them in. I think I will sign both of us up to go to the range in Conklin and practice."

"I know that you have been worried about the state of the economy and our finances. Are you okay? Things will get better you know. America has been through bad times before. We went through a really bad time but we survived. Things are getting better."

He looked at his smart, pretty wife in the growing twilight. He had always secretly counted himself very lucky having Sam as his wife. She was an attractive woman. She kept herself in good shape. She was healthy, with nice curves, and intelligent. When he met her fourteen years ago she was the assistant manager at a huge advertising firm in New York City. When she made the transition to Binghamton she actually took a massive pay cut to manage a small satellite branch. It had seemed even with that pay cut that they were pretty secure until the second post-2007 recession hit. It was a remarkable thing how she decided to switch her career. Going for something completely new, she went back to school and two years later was a nurse. So Alfi, knowing that his wife always saw the glass as half full, understood that she would have a positive spin on the dour times.

He decided then and there that he was not going to lie to his wife even if she did not share his view on things. "Well I don't know Sam, the more I see things and read about things, the more worried I get. I keep telling myself the same thing. Things will get better, everything will work out. America is just too big and powerful to fail. But I see all these stories now about how the banks are failing, or losing massive amounts of money through bad investments, and countries in Europe tanking and I don't know what to believe anymore. I keep telling myself that we have a lot of really smart people in this country; they will figure a way out of this mess. But it just seems like we are on a train, barreling down the tracks and there is no engineer to put the brakes on, and waiting at the end of the line is a really solid concrete wall." He sighed. "I am just going to make some preparations just in case."

"So are you saying then that there will be another massive recession and that there will be anarchy in the streets? Because it will never get to that you know. I could see us sliding into another recession of course. But, our jobs are pretty much recession proof at this point. I am a nurse, always in demand and you are a quality manager at the plant. This city will never let that factory fold. You know why, it feeds more than the thousand people on its payroll. All the local farmers who have gone seriously into dairy production, to meet its demands, need it. All the local businesses that supply materials need it, and so the plant isn't going anywhere. As far as I can see, we should be able to ride this thing out, if it comes."

Alfi smiled at his wife, and in the darkening light it came across as a wistfully grim look. "Well what I will do is just make sure that if we need to hole up here at home, in an emergency, we will be okay, for at least a couple of weeks." Samantha then understood that her

husband was like a man with an itch he had to scratch. She realized that although she did not agree with his take on things, the healthiest thing she could do was let him scratch the itch. Things were bad enough without them adding tension to their marriage. She was not worried about money; Alfi was cautious with their money. She did the books and she was sure that if he was going to make a big purchase, it would get run by her first, to see if they could afford it. So although she didn't agree and although she knew she would be the one voicing her dissent about the state of things, she said "Do what you feel you have to do. I guess the way we can look at it is that it could be a sort of insurance policy. One that I hope we never have to cash in."
It was after this conversation, one that Alfred would remember years later; he could really say that he became a true prepper.
*

He acted quickly. Like a man taking a dip into cold icy water he sort of mentally gritted his teeth and plunged right in. The following day after work Alfi went to the local sports store and bought the first of what would turn out to be weapons of necessity. He bought a Henry .22 Long Rifle and two 12 gauge Mossberg tactical shot guns. The next day he called the local gun club, and found out about their membership requirements. That weekend he drove over and signed himself and his wife up.

The following Wednesday after work, they drove to the range to really check out the facilities and to try their hand at shooting. The people that they met were friendly but a bit distant; Alfi attributed this to the fact that they were new members. They went out to the rifle range and there they carefully learned how to load and unload the weapons safely, and also how to use the correct eye to aim and shoot.

Samantha found that contrary to her expectations she really enjoyed the experience, and she couldn't wait to do it again. They found that with the .22 rifle she was a better shot than Alfi. They found themselves making plans to come back the following week to practice some more. Samantha also realized that the weapons were tools, dangerous ones that should be treated with respect and care. They would always be locked away in the safe that Alfi had purchased.

On the ride home from the range, Alfred decided that he would purchase his fishing license and he would sign up to take a hunter safety course in the fall. He figured if there was ever a problem he would make sure he could hunt 'legally.' It might come in handy with any law enforcement agency encounter. He also decided to get some mace for their home. Now mace or pepper spray was not illegal in Upstate New York, but one had to go to a special pharmacy or store that sold it, to fill out the paperwork required by law.

That night after doing some research he found a pharmacy that sold the stuff. It was sixty miles from his house. He would be going for a little drive tomorrow, after work. In Alfi's mind what he was doing was taking care of the 'able to defend home' part of his check list. There were still a few items to acquire, but he estimated between getting pistol permits and saving enough money to buy the rest of the guns—a couple of Ruger Mini14s rifles and two .38 revolvers—it would take at least another year. In the meantime he had the basic necessities, three guns for home protection and hunting.

It was also surprising to Samantha that she found herself feeling better knowing that they had the mace which they kept in a box by the bed. It was nice knowing that when Alfi was out she could defend the children and herself with some serious intent and vigor. Alfi had done some practice squeezes and some of the liquid had come back his way, real rookie mistake. He had come rushing into the house, running for the tap, so they knew it worked. And they also learned that they would have to make sure they got the attacker and not themselves. She went to the pharmacy and bought a cute pink bottle of the stuff for her purse.
*

Alfi began turning his mind to other things. There was still a lot to do, and he decided then that food was going to be next. He wanted a thirty day food supply for his family. He also decided to take the advice of the writers who advised to stock up on the things you like to eat instead of MRE's or food that was dehydrated. Food would be important in maintaining morale. So began his great stocking spree. He began by stocking a variety of canned fruits and vegetables. Then he moved onto canned meats and soups. He stocked the basics; rice, sugar, potatoes, ultra pasteurized and powdered milk, coffee, tea, flour, eggs, cornmeal, oatmeal, and powdered drinks. He stacked up on alcohol, rum, vodka, and whisky. Potassium iodine tablets, sanitary napkins, toilet paper, painkillers, birth control items, his supply list went on and on. He then filled his freezer with as much meat as it could hold. He carefully labeled everything so that he could eat the oldest food first, to prevent waste, then all he had to do was to replace whatever they ate. He also kept a small supply of sweets around, for the kids he told himself.

With the filling of the freezer he then knew the time had come to get a generator. At first as he researched the best way to power his home in an emergency, he just thought he would get the cheapest, most reliable gas model he could find. However the more he looked into it he realized that in an emergency, gas was going to be scarce. He read about a gas-propane hybrid, which appealed to him. Propane was a good alternative. It was just easier to store and the propane generators seem to have less mechanical problems. Then he started to think about solar power. He reckoned that if the grid was to go down for any reason, then maybe not needing to use any kind of fuel to run the basic household items might be the best option. It would cost him more now, but the savings down the road would be immense. He could then use his stash of fuel for other things.

He invested in a Sunrnr system. He had an electrician install the panels on his roof, and the inverter and extra power module in his basement. The cost while high was not as prohibitive as he thought because he got a bit of help from the government, in terms of loans, since he was installing a solar power system. He decided on the grid tie to save on his electric bill, but if the power went out the system would automatically kick on. He also made sure that he could completely disconnect from NYSEG whenever he wanted to. After extensive research he and Samantha realized that if they really wanted to they could live off the grid completely. They would just have to be cautious with their fuel consumption, that's all.

With the installation of the solar system, Alfi began to feel a whole lot better. He had gotten a long way in his preps. He had made strides in home defense, food and emergency power. Now he had to see about first aid. Samantha, being a nurse, created a small stash of antibiotics and emergency trauma supplies. It was in this way that Alfi continued in his preps, unaware of the attention he had attracted to himself. So it was with some surprise, when he came home one evening from work, that he found an NSA officer sitting in his living room having a cup of tea. The man's name was Lambert. He wore a nicely tailored dark suit which made his presence even more unnerving. Alfred had heard about the NSA spying on US Citizens, since the Snowden Affair years ago. It still came as a shock that he had attracted that kind of special attention to himself.

Lambert had at his feet a small elegant leather attaché case. After shaking Alfi's hand and introducing himself, he sat down on the couch in front of the coffee table. He smiled and said,

"Hi Alfred, I am agent Lambert from the Southern Tier Homeland Security Division. It is our job to monitor all suspicious activity here in the Broome County area. Now I don't want to alarm you but I just want to inform you and your wife that your activity has raised a few red flags."

"What do you mean?" Samantha asked.

"Well your husband's internet use and your bank account activity have raised a few concerns." He reached down and started to take some papers from the attaché case. Alfi realized that he had two files in his hand. "Now these documents are one, internet traffic, and two, bank activity. We noticed that you have been going to a few web sites we have flagged." He placed the files on the coffee table and began to sift through the papers. "Now we noticed that you have become a frequent reader of *Survivor Prepper*, *Last Man Standing* and the *Real News.com*." He looked at Alfi with a perplexed frown.

"Yeah, I have been reading those websites for the past year or so. The people who post just seem to have some good ideas on how to be more self-reliant."

"Really, self-reliant, what do you mean by that exactly?"

"Well it just seems like a lot of the people who post on those blogs, seem to know a lot about how to prepare and get by during a disaster."

"Ohh... and are you expecting a disaster Mr. Aimes?"

"Well after the massive floods we had here in Binghamton I realized that I was not ready. If something was to happen that knocked out the electricity or we were cut off because of a massive snow storm, we would get by, but we would be running it awfully close. Too close for my liking."

"Ohh, but don't most people just have a few cans of extra food and a medical kit around in case of an emergency? If there is an emergency, the government will get help to those who need it in a timely way. That's what most sane Americans do."

"Well I am of the opinion that if there is an emergency, the less people needing help from the government, the better. You wouldn't have to give your precious resources to me. My family and I would be one less problem."

"That's where I think a lot of people are mistaken. These people who claim to be experts, who hoard food and gasoline, will not be looking out for their fellow citizens. It is the pinnacle of selfishness and narcissism. These are usually the people who get in the way of law and order. They will not help their fellow man. It's all about them and their narcissistic dreams. A lot of these people are hoping that something bad does happen so they can be proven right."

Lambert was looking at Alfred closely as he said this. His words made Alfi smile. "Well I don't know about all of that, Agent Lambert. I know that you must see some truly bad people in your line of work. I just want to have the peace of mind to know that if something did occur my family would be able to ride it out, at least for a little while."

"What about your neighbors Mr. Aimes? Would you be helping your neighbors if there was indeed an emergency of some kind?"

"Well I would try to do as much as I could, without putting myself and my family at risk."

"But isn't a hero someone who goes above and beyond? Someone who does a selfless act for the benefit of others?"

"Samantha, I am sure you and the kids want me around for a really long time. Do you want me to be a hero?" Alfred smiled.

"If you are putting your life on the line for the kids and me, well sure. For someone else, no, I would like to think that we come first. Your family needs you. I do not need a hero for a husband."

"I noticed that you bought three firearms, a .22 Long Rifle and two 12 Gauge shotguns. You have never owned a gun all your lives, both of you. Why would you want to own them now? Why bring that danger into your household?"

"Well the decision wasn't taken lightly," Alfred said, "But it was something that I had been thinking about for a long time. The first thing we looked at, agent, was where we live. It's a really nice community out here, but the homes are kind of isolated, and we are not close to any town. If we were to pick up the phone to call for help from any law enforcement agency, the quickest they would get here is probably ten to fifteen minutes. A lot can happen in ten to fifteen minutes. We decided that we needed a way to take care of ourselves, getting the guns and the mace was a way to do that. I feel a lot better now knowing that if I am at work, Samantha has a way of defending herself and the kids. Plus I do intend on going hunting one of these days as well."

"Well what if one of the kids gets a hold of one of these weapons, and accidentally shoots him or herself, a friend, or, God forbid, one of you?"

"Well the guns are locked up and the ammunition is in a place where only Sam and I know."

Lambert eyed Alfi through a calculating wrinkled gaze. "Well as I said Mr. and Mrs. Aimes, your internet and bank account has raised a lot of red flags. I guess you are just another one of those so called preppers, or survivalists, who think that something bad is going to happen."

"I don't know about that," Alfred countered. "We just think that the important functions of the home and the adults living in the home happens to include being able to put food on the table in good or bad times, as well as protecting their children and loved ones. When you can't do that your world just falls apart."

Lambert packed up his paperwork and after a polite reference to the lovely cup of tea Sam had given him, he left their home. After cleaning up and checking on the kids Samantha took Alfi's hand in the kitchen and said quietly, "I may not agree with you about the state of affairs in this country. But I do agree with your underlying motives, which is to keep us safe." Alfi breathed out a sigh of relief because he didn't know how she would take Lambert's visit. He was just glad that she didn't side with Lambert against him.

Alfi was to continue his preps unabated for the next two years. In the meantime he got his hunting license and went hunting with some guys he met at the range. They showed him how to track and prepare the deer after it was shot. It was something he really wanted to experience and learn.

He and Samantha also got their conceal carry permits. He went out and bought two .38 revolvers. The .38s were safer to check and clean, and easier to aim and shoot than other options. They were also small enough to carry concealed. He continued to stock his pantry, and he also learned how to operate a ham radio. So Alfi found that between his family, job, and prepping, his life was full. He felt better knowing that as far as he could make out, they were as self-sufficient as he could make them. This would get tested when the troubles started.

Chapter Two: SHTF

"There is no greater grief than to remember days of joy when misery is at hand". Dante Alighieri

A few years later:
The way the meltdown began caught most by surprise. It wasn't just one main event; it was a combination of four things, the war with Iran, the terrorist group Al –Qaeda, the uncertain world economy, and a really bad year for farmers all combined to drag the world under. Alfi watched as the USA's confrontation with Iran slowly escalated. It was not the rest of the world's problem as much as it was America's problem. At a time when there was a real need to be concerned with what an unstable power was doing with its nuclear program, the rest of the world had bigger things on their mind. Their economies were tanking or had tanked. First it was Greece, and then Spain, then Italy and finally the entire European continent slowly slipped into the jaws of deep fiscal depression. There was a lot of rioting and civil unrest and in some countries the institution of martial law.

It was interesting that when the American crash, or what later on was called 'The Collapse', came; it caught most unaware, even Alfi. He watched as the Iranian problem escalated and deescalated. One minute it seemed like the Iranians had pushed too far and then they would draw back. This fiasco went on for a time. One more President came and went. The US economy just kept on getting worse. The hole was just too deep. No matter how many jobs were created and the small rise in the GDP, the USA could not catch up to its spiraling debt.

Then one day Alfi was at work when he saw the flash of a headline online. Israel had attacked Iran, bombing suspected nuclear targets. When he had gotten home that evening, he switched on the news and watched as most of the world condemned the Israeli raids. The Israelis had apparently gotten sick of the rest of the world, including the United States, pussy footing around, while Iran lied and carried on its nuclear program. The Iranians threatened retaliation.

And boy how they retaliated! Twenty four hours later they lobbed two nuclear tipped ballistic missiles into Israel. The result was the devastation of the cities of Tel Aviv and Jerusalem, with the death toll somewhere in the vicinity of 90 thousand, with more to come from radiation exposure. Alfi felt a chill go up his spine, and as he and Sam watched the world fragmenting he knew things would never be the same again.
*

They watched as CNN showed pictures and clips of the mushroom clouds. There was even footage coming out of the devastated areas taken from private cell phones. The President came on later that night to say that the Iranians would not go unpunished. The following day Samantha insisted that the kids not go to school. He saw the logic in that and did not object. They agreed that she would call if anything went down and if the phones were out she could get in touch with him with the CB's they had installed in their cars.

Alfi went to work that day feeling apprehensive. The Iranian nuclear attack was all his fellow co-workers were chatting about. Radios and computers were tuned into the news networks as the day wore on. What had surprised Alfi as well as everyone else was the harsh reality that one country had used nuclear weapons against another. Something that had not been done since the United States had bombed Japan. Alfi had the unsettling feeling that this act had kicked the lid off the proverbial Pandora's Box. The mad men had used nuclear weapons without any regard to what the consequences would be to them or their neighboring countries. Apart from the horrifying death toll and devastation, the scientists were now trying to figure out where the fallout was going. It did seem that most of it was going to descend on the countries surrounding Israel, who were the Iranians' allies. The rash act would doom countless others to a life of sickness, deformity, and death.

That evening Alfi went to his gun safe, opened it and eyed his growing gun collection. He had purchased two Ruger Mini 14 tactical rifles, instead of the AR rifles he had wanted but were unavailable in New York State. Most gun stores had pulled them off the shelves in reaction to a new horrible shooting in Sylvester, New Jersey. He remembered how years after the first Governor assault weapons ban—one that was fought in the courts relentlessly and then eventually repealed— that he had gone to his usual gun store. He realized that the rifles he wanted were no longer in stock. When he asked Jasper, what would be adequate protection, the clerk, a fellow member of his gun club and occasional hunting partner, smiled and with a twinkle in his eyes said, "I knew you had an eye on the Mini 14s. I know you said you wouldn't be able to afford it but it's amazing what another impending gun ban can do. And believe it, this Governor just like all his predecessors and his cronies are going to use this new tragedy to further his political aspirations, yessir you can count on that. I had been keeping a few in back. Just give me a second."

Jasper, a small stocky man with short curly red hair, went to the storage room and came back with two boxes that held the Minis. He took one of the guns out of the box and snapped it together. He showed Alfi how to load and fire. He gave him two 10 round clips and five hundred rounds of ammunition. "Take them to the range or to your back yard and practice firing and loading. Make sure your wife gets some practice as well. I kept these off the shelves because of all the so-called gun aficionados who would be coming in to buy weapons, before the ban comes into place. These I am only selling to fellow preppers, who I know will use common sense."

Alfi looked at him dumbfounded. Jasper still had that enigmatic smile on his face. "I can recognize a prepper a mile away, and don't worry about it. I know these guns are in good hands; hopefully you won't have to ever use 'em." Alfi then filled out the paper work and left sometime later with his firearms. As he drove home Jasper's words came back to him and he felt a bit queasy in his stomach. The following day he and Samantha went into the back yard and practiced with their new guns. In retrospect he thanked his lucky stars that he had put up with the opportunist Governor's new unconstitutional so called assault weapons ban and registered his guns every year. But in light of current events he was thankful that he had the additional fire power, just in case.
*

The tragedy that started what would be called in history the "Great Gun Grab of the Early 21st Century" was shocking and mind numbing. But what really appalled Alfred was how the politicians pandered to the fears of the people to push through legislations that they knew right then would do nothing to stem the violence. The scales had already been tipping since the horrible tragedy at Newtown years ago, and public opinion had finally swung the way of the gun control advocates after an even worse shooting at a place called Sylvester in New Jersey. He was appalled at how the 'Righteous Media' on both sides of the debate slanted the news to further their own agendas. The media were becoming active participants in the news stories they covered, pushing their own beliefs. He watched in uneasy fascination as biased media talking heads on both sides of the issue were given unlimited airtime to push their agendas.

He noticed how one station would show anti-gun demonstrations while making no mention of the pro-gun demonstrators and visa versa. He saw how the media turned the AR15 into a gun of almost supernatural malevolence. He perceived how they created the myth of the gun and he realized that every mad man or psychopath intent on a killing would now search for this mythical weapon. By linking it, and focusing on it when it was used in horrible crimes committed by madmen, it was now the weapon of choice for other psychopaths. The media themselves were complicit and they would never own it. They would not understand the harm they themselves were committing.

He would groan every time they called it a machine gun, every time they said it was a gun for the military only. He knew that the AR was a semi-automatic rifle. He knew that no soldier would go into action with a semi-automatic rifle because they would be outgunned by the enemy carrying fully automatic select fire weapons. He groaned when he heard the argument which said that fully automatic weapons were banned, so why should semi-automatics not be banned. Well he thought that banning the autos was unconstitutional. It had paved the way for the gradual chipping away of the 2nd Amendment. He groaned whenever he heard the term 'gun violence' because the guns never fired themselves, it was always a person, man, woman, child that pulled the trigger. It took the blame away from the person and placed it on the weapon.

He saw how the Progressives, when they met any opposition to their agenda, would say to their opponents that the blood of the children was on their hands. They charged that their opponents did not care about the safety of children, which was horrifically false. He knew that new car standards, which made them lighter to meet fuel mileage requirements, killed way more people every year than guns, and maimed a whole lot more. Heck the leakage of the Fukushima Nuclear Plant into the Pacific all those years probably had given millions cancer and killed millions around the world and in the US, but no one really cared or talked about that. But the arguments were lost in the heated rhetoric.

Alfred saw himself not anti gun or pro gun. He did though see firearms as an unfortunately necessary thing in the world. He refused to bury his head in the sand. In Alfred's way of thinking about things, and the gun owners that he knew, he realized that he would trust those people not to rob and murder more than the ones without guns. The ones without legal guns always

seemed to be able to find ways to kill each other, in way greater numbers than the individuals who legally owned fire arms. Most of the crimes in which guns were used were committed by people who obtained their firearms illegally.
*

He remembered years ago, after the Sylvester massacre, how he had written a letter to the then Governor and he went upstairs to his computer and switched it on. He had been in a state of deep concern as he wrote the letter that he had emailed to the Governor. He had saved a copy of a draft to his computer, and now he pulled it up and read it.

Dear Sir,

I am very troubled about this new anti gun law I have read about that is about to be proposed by you. I and the country are very shocked at the horror that madman perpetrated on those families in Sylvester. I am very concerned that anti gun opponents will and are using this horrible tragedy to drive us further away from the true meaning and value of the second amendment. I am not a Republican, I consider myself a Progressive in most things. But I get a bit squeamish when I see government officials tampering around with our Constitution; it's a really slippery slope. We meet a law that's a bit of an inconvenience and we amend and tweak and finally we overturn.

Anti gun proponents argue that the founding fathers didn't mean for citizens to have guns that are so powerful, but I would counter that with the argument that citizens at the time were armed with guns that were equal to what the armies had at the time. The average US citizen is already at a disadvantage. We hear about those horrible home invasions where the family or homeowner is killed, and usually those citizens did not have a means of protecting themselves. Law enforcement in those situations always arrives after the worst is done.

I think they (The Founding Fathers) would want to move with the times. We have gotten lost in the weeds here. Disarming the public is not only a personal safety issue but a national security issue as well. While the odds are very slim that we would ever have to face the hypothetical prospect of an invasion by a foreign enemy, the fact is that a well-armed populace would be very instrumental to the defending of this country. The United States of America is a very large country. If an enemy were to drop troops, strategically in different parts of the country to do harm, intent on capturing and holding certain areas, our great military would be stretched to fight a war like that. They would need the help of the citizens in and around the areas of trouble. Remember the war we fought in Afghanistan years ago, a country that is roughly the size of Texas. We expended an enormous amount of financial resources, troops, and equipment to prosecute that war. Imagine a scenario where we have to fight an enemy in 15 or 20 of our States. Could our military deal with something on that scale?

If they know that there are not a lot of gun owners in New York then it becomes an even more inviting target. We would all have to rely completely on the Armed forces to get the job done. Now while this hypothetical scenario is remote, and some people may even see it as paranoia instead of a hypothetical situation, it does however serve the purpose of showing there are sometimes unintentional negative results from tampering with the Constitution. Government officials *are sometimes a bit smug, when they are reminded that they are sworn in to uphold and protect that very Constitution. They ignore it and instead push their own private dogmas. That I find troubling as a citizen because it makes our government ineffective as per what's going on in Washington now with regards to the economic issues they need to fix.*

New York does not need any more gun laws. Officials need to properly enforce the laws that are already on the books. They need to put into place a national database of people with mental problems so these people cannot get hold of weapons. I do believe that people who intend to do others harm as in the case of the Sylvester madman, with his rifles and pressure cooker bombs, will just find other ways to commit mass murder. I agree that gun owners should be made to take a gun safety course before purchasing their first gun. I don't understand the hypocrisy of government officials who make the gun laws tougher while they either have armed security or are themselves armed. There seems to be a double standard there, are they more valuable than the average citizen? I cannot see the point in further disarming law abiding citizens when the criminals will become better armed themselves.

In closing I would just like to say although I am just a voice of one. I will look to see which politicians vote on these laws to prevent citizens from owning guns, and they will not get my vote during the next election cycle. Alfred Aimes.

Reading that letter brought back a lot of memories now. He was glad that he had acted despite what he knew were going to be registration and certifying inconveniences. He felt a whole lot better with those guns in the house. He hoped to God that he would not have to use them.

*

Scanning the television stations and internet yielded little in terms of what the US and its Allies were going to do about the Iranian situation. Three days later they had their answer. The Americans were forced to go it alone, and they launched an attack on Iranian targets from a couple of Aircraft carriers that had steamed into the Gulf. This happened in the early morning. Alfi listened to the details as he drove to work. The American planes destroyed nuclear targets within the country. This sparked a rise in the cost of oil, all across the globe. Countries that were just hanging on cracked.

When he got to work he went online, rules be damned, and he read about the massive run on the banks in Europe, Russia, and Asia. People had completely lost faith in the banking institutions and were pulling their money out. They were also making a run on their local supermarkets, stocking up on food. The NASDAQ sagged, and then dropped like a rock. By the end of the week several big banks like Morgan Stanley and Citibank announced that they were in danger of becoming insolvent. They had taken huge blows in investments from which there was no coming back.

*

That weekend Alfie and Sam had a few friends over for dinner. This was something they had planned for a while and thought it was a good idea not to cancel. The two couples they had invited were old friends.

Peter and Janice Pywoski were both real estate agents, and the other couple, Benjamin and Peggy Green, ran a plumbing business. They sat at the dinner table; Peter the most extroverted of the group had them in stitches. There was a lot to catch up on. Peggy asked off handedly about the panels on the roof. "Ohh we decided to have a way of getting emergency power just in case there ever was an outage. We went solar, got to be green you know." Samantha replied with a grin. After dessert was served, the friends retired to the living room. It was mid June and the evening was unseasonably cool. It was too chilly to sit on the porch.

The television was on, the volume was very low, but they could all see the pictures of the people rioting in the streets, and it reminded Alfi of the riots that had taken place years ago in the Middle East during the so called 'Arab Spring'. This particular riot was in the streets of Iraq. The angry protesters were shouting "Death to America."

"Well doesn't that beat all? We got rid of Saddam Hussein and help bring them democracy, their neighbor drops two nuclear missiles on another country, and now all the surrounding countries are dealing with the fallout and they blame us? Is the world insane or what?" Benjamin, a small thin man with thinning blond hair, remarked.

"Yeah I just have a feeling that something's going to happen, you know. This thing that has begun is just rippling around the world. It's going to suck us in. It always sucks us in." Peggy added. There was a general consensus on that point. The mood of the party became a bit grim.

"How is the housing market?" Alfi asked.

"It's bad and getting worse. So many people are selling. They have either been laid off or just fired. This has all the earmarking of the Depression of 2007 written all over it again." Janice remarked.

"No I think it'll be a lot worse this time," Benjamin interjected. "I think we've built a house of cards and it will all come tumbling down soon."

"Why would you say that? I mean the country has gone through tough times before, and we have bounced back." Peter said trying to keep things light. It didn't work, and the mood had now shifted from levity to somberness.

Benjamin sipped his beer and said "Well let's put it this way. We never really got ourselves out of the hole we got ourselves into in the first place. They ripped out the guts of this country. They lied to us, all those goddamn politicians. They lied to us and now most of them have taken their fat retirement plans and corporate payoffs and have left us holding an empty bag." He looked over at his wife, who had a smirk on her face. "You guys know I hear this all the time right." She reached over and squeezed his hand.

He shifted in his seat away from her, to face the others more squarely. "You guys can smirk all you want you know what I am saying is true. I can feel it in my bones that something is coming. Did anyone see that movie *Take Shelter* when that guy had those dreams or premonitions that something bad was coming, well that's how I feel. I feel trapped and I don't know what to do about it. Our oldest kid Christopher just got a job with some big firm in Philadelphia, and our daughter is doing well, psychiatry is booming at the moment. So I should be looking at my family and saying that I am blessed, but that isn't the case. I keep looking over my shoulder because something just isn't right."

"Well I know just what you mean." Alfi said with a sigh. "With all the stuff going on, when you look at the crises in the Middle East and the problems going

on with the banks and our economy, it is very unsettling. The only thing I can tell you my friends is that if you feel something isn't right, if you feel that something bad is coming our way, then you need to look at your lives and hope for the best but prepare for the worst." He smiled, and looked at his friends in the soft glow of the living room lights. They talked about more politics and then moved on to happier subjects. It was the last time they would all be together.
*

    It was 5 am on a Friday morning, and Alfi got up to use the bathroom. While he was peeing, his bathroom window lit up in a kaleidoscope of flashing lights. He heard two heavy vehicles fly by. Then three more cars went by. This was unprecedented on Pine Road where they were lucky if a single car went by in an hour. As he got up from the toilet, he felt something go cold in his stomach. He turned on the television. The horrible news just rushed out at him, grabbing him tight by the throat. It dragged him over to the couch and he watched the unbelievable story unfolding in horrid fascination.

    There had been four coordinated suitcase nuclear attacks on US soil. Alfi looked on as they showed the footage of two of the small nuclear plumes. The other two attacks were not caught by any news organization, but the reporters were sure that there would be amateur film of the events available soon. The cities attacked were all soft targets, Syracuse, New York; Topeka, Kansas; Kokomo, Indiana; and Redding, California. The devices' yields were powerful enough that great portions of the cities were destroyed.

    The real extent of the damage and loss of life was not yet known. There were also reports of similar attacks in England, Germany, and China. Alfi was unaware of the time passing, and Samantha got up and came down to see what was wrong. She sat down beside him on the couch. "This is absolutely nuts," he said, his voice sounding raspy and dry.

"Ohh my God! Ohh my God!" Sam kept saying over and over again. Alfi switched to CNN, the reporter a grim faced man in his late fifties was giving the bad news to the watching American public:

"Ladies and gentlemen, we are witness to an unprecedented attack against the US. An attack of such magnitude that Pearl Harbor pales in comparison. It pales because of the scope, it pales because of the loss of human life, and it pales because nuclear weapons were used. Never before has an enemy struck such a crushing and mortal blow on our soil. We know from good sources that the attacks were most likely the heretofore theoretical suitcase bombs. It is believed that all the attacks were carried out by suicide bombers. All the targets were smaller American cities which were never thought of being symbolically important enough for the terrorist groups to target. The estimated casualty list now coming in stands at a presumed 300 thousand dead, with another 150 thousand badly injured or poisoned by the radiation. Homes, businesses, and infrastructure in and around the blast zones in those cities have been utterly destroyed."

"This has been a nightmare for first responders, because of the difficulty in traversing an active radioactive zone. The President is set to speak to the nation live in just under an hour. I am sure he is being briefed with the latest information. It has also been reported to CNN that the secret service has moved the President, Vice President, and his cabinet members to secret hardened locations." He paused and looked at a piece of paper that was shoved into his hand. "This just coming in that the President has signed into effect martial law for all 50 states. The only personnel allowed to move about are military and police, and other emergency personnel. Until further notice all citizens must remain in their homes or within the environs of their property until the curfew is lifted."

Alfred felt the world collapsing around him. There was a surreal quality to it all. The emotion he realized he was feeling was confusion, even more than anger, or fright, that was the overwhelming emotion. Samantha looked pale and fragile in her sleep shirt. "Jesus, who could have done this? The world is going mad." She reached for Alfi's hand and they sat there and watched the horrible news unfold. Time slipped by and it seemed like they had held their collective breath, and when they finally exhaled, the warm June sun had begun to shine through the living room's windows.

They watched the President's speech. It was odd how seeing the Commander in Chief made them feel better. All around America right now, Alfi realized that people just like them, normal families, men and women, people who could not rightly be called Republicans or Democrats, Conservatives or Liberals, watched the President and felt hope. Order was still present, the country was still there. The Justice Department would be looking into the attacks; the perpetrators would be found and punished. After the President finished his address to the nation, Samantha got up and went into the kitchen to make coffee.
*

Alfred realized then that their two teenage children were still sleeping in. Sitting there on the sofa the thought of his children turned his blood to ice. 'What kind of a world were they waking up to now?' Robert was a bright fifteen year old who had been looking forward to driving lessons and Candice now thirteen was actually looking forward to getting out of the Middle School Hell this year, as she had termed it.

He felt it in his bones that something had been irretrievably lost. The world he had grown up in was fading away into the twilight, and a new one was being born. His children had just slept through one of the most significant events in world history, and when they woke up, it would be a new world, a very uncertain world. Not knowing what to do Alfi went online. It was amazing that the internet was still working. He then saw that most cell phone service was almost nonexistent. People online complained that the internet was slow. He didn't notice much of a difference, at first. He tried the big newspapers, *The New York Times* and *The Washington Post*, to see if he could get more information, but he could not get on. He eventually settled for the stories on his *Yahoo* and *Google* pages. These just regurgitated what he already saw earlier on the television.

He then went onto a few of the prepper websites he visited regularly and saw that they all had run stories on the attack. The stories were covered differently than in the main stream media. Most were written giving the facts of the attack, along with hints of what might happen next. That was the main difference between the mainstream media and the prepper blogs. There were some very interesting hypothetical scenarios, as to what the government would do, as well as the terrorists. What all this made Alfi realize was that the attack was just the tip of the iceberg. A lot more was going to come down the pipe. Questions were asked on the blogs as to how this was going to affect an already failing economy.

The cities where the attacks had taken place were now effectively Dead Zones. How America would react to the attacks was another important question making the rounds. It was then he also realized that now given that the worst case scenario had occurred many people were praying that it could somehow be fixed. Most preppers did not want the world to go to pieces. They had families and loved ones, lives, they enjoyed. These things would be threatened and probably lost for good if America fell apart.

There were some people however who were relishing the chaos. They were praying for the collapse of the world order. This just seemed insane to Alfi. For in his mind, he had a vivid flash of insight, the trailing end of a disturbing vision in which he saw fire and desolation, over vast areas of the country. It was a world he did not want any part of. The racist elements of the community were in full swing with their rants about everyone who was non-white. That really rankled Alfi. Because he realized that the country he was living in had created a lot of its own problems. It had shaped a lot of its young people. A disturbing majority had become self-absorbed narcissists, with very little, if any, empathy. And it wasn't just the young; it was also those die hard end of the world preppers.

What Alfi hated was the practice of the narcissist ideology. They existed in their own worlds, convinced that they were always right. They were convinced that they had insights that others didn't, that they were somehow outside the chain links of humanity. Those were the people who did not care for human life. They only looked out for themselves and only wanted to be right. They scared Alfi. They did not realize that the problems that were showcased by the mainstream media, the same media they accused as being biased and slanted, were everybody's problems. It amazed Alfi that a lot of these people could not see that what was shown happening in one ethnic community, or another city's neighborhood, was also happening in their communities as well. But it made them feel superior, to think that where they lived, or within their circle they were safe from the evils of the world. Alfi realized that just as there were good, there were a lot of bad people everywhere, and race, ethnicity, gender, or sexual orientation did not matter a jot, on that score.

A lot of the people who left comments on the boards thought that they would survive a full societal collapse. Alfi knew better. He had a wonderful wife and two teenage children, whom he wanted to see grow up and have happy lives. He wanted no part of Armageddon. It was then he also realized just what he would do to protect his family. He realized that his life and main aim was to preserve the lives of the ones he loved. He understood this with a sharp clarity he had not known even during the years he had spent prepping.

Just like everyone, he had his suspicions as to what organization may have committed the attacks. It seemed like a foregone conclusion. It was even being reported on most of the news networks that the attacks were carried out by Al-Qaida. A couple of days after the attacks spotty details emerged. It seemed that the terrorists had infiltrated the country, through the porous Mexican border and had gone on directly to attack their targets. The stealthy radicalization going on south of our borders had gone by mostly ignored until now.

A lot of the news agencies were also linking Iran to the attacks. This seemed to be confirmed when the President got the Congress's approval to completely minimize the Iranian threat. Three weeks after the attacks, America went to war in a way not seen in a generation. This was not a distant war for the citizens, as Iraq and Afghanistan had been. It was short, awesome and brutal.

For the first time America went to war, not caring what the rest of the world would think. In less than 20 days Iran was no longer a threat to anyone. Four intercontinental ballistic nuclear missiles fired from submarines in the Persian Gulf ended any resistance. What really surprised Alfi was the silence from the world community after the attacks. No one wanted any of it. They understood the stakes, when the US started firing nuclear missiles. Something monumental had shifted on the world's stage. As it turned out, the 20 day war would be the last meaningful military engagement carried out by the Americans for the next 10 years.
*

Three months after the attacks, martial law was lifted. America, like a pummeled prize fighter, refused to go down. It swayed and teetered but stayed on its feet. The country had absorbed a great amount of punishment. People began to believe again. They figured that Uncle Sam had survived the worst that its enemies could throw at it and had come through. They had the belief that the people would come together and make things work. But as it turned out it was a bit too late. While the war had spurred a momentary feeling of optimism, in Europe there was a full blown panic going on, one that finally broke the worlds' financial system. One by one the countries went under. The Middle East was in flames from the wars, and oil prices finally sent the European Union crashing. Most of the African, South American and Caribbean countries were either in the midst of wars, coups, or desperately trying to stave off the complete collapse of their fragile infrastructures. Suddenly people realized that their money wasn't worth the paper it was printed on. When it crashed, the US, China, and Russia followed suit.

Because he was actually paying attention to the correct things in the media, Alfred was aware of what was happening. More than anything, it was perhaps that he had already been preparing which made him feel capable of helping himself. Alfi had gone into supper prepper mode in the last three months (July-Sept) before The World Financial Crash or what would be later called, 'The Collapse.' Samantha no longer needed to be convinced. She had seen the news and understood that there was no way they were going to come through unscathed. They contacted Peter and Janice Pywoski. Alfi arranged for them to purchase a 96 acre plot of land. It was a parcel of land that the Pywoskis had been trying for close to a year to offload, but no one wanted it. When Alfi inquired about a property away from any heavily inhabited towns and close to a state park, for ultimate privacy reasons, they had just the parcel he had been looking for.

Samantha wrote the check for 55 thousand dollars herself. Alfi then leased a bulldozer and cleared a path into the woods about a quarter mile from the road. He then hired an Amish company to drop a small hunting log cabin in a clearing he had made; he arranged for a contractor to put in a well and installed a hand pump.

He had the water tested for radiation contamination and found that the levels were normal. It was all done under the guise that he was creating a hunting lodge for himself and four friends. When the well was done he dropped four metal containers around the cabin, forming a larger square outer perimeter. He and Sam took about a month off from work and worked every day on *The Rabbit Hole*, their christened name for their bug out location.

They bought enough emergency rations to last them a few months, and seeds. He bought the solar panels himself and installed them on and around the cabin and hooked them into an array of rechargeable 12 volt batteries. It was with great satisfaction that he realized that he would have enough power to run a small radio and refrigerator, and recharge small appliances and batteries for tools. They bought small cheap solar lamps that they could leave out and recharge in the sun. They stocked up on gasoline as well at the new location. He also began buying lots of ammunition for his guns, which was tough because everyone was doing the same and there was a severe shortage. He purchased two Ruger M77 Hawkeye Magnum Hunter rifles and two Colt .45 pistols. He kept one of the .45s for himself and buried the rest of the firearms on the property. They allowed the access track Alfi had cleared with the dozer to become overgrown so it was not visible from the road. Two months after they started, they felt that if there was an emergency and they could not go home or were forced to leave their home, they had someplace safe to stay.

They told no one about their arrangements. They also traded in Samantha's Toyota Camry for a used Chevy Tahoe. They took the children up to *The Rabbit*

Hole to get used to it and they did. At first it was a bit tentative. It had none of the technological amenities they were used to, but they understood that it was supposed to be a place of safety for the family. Their parents also made them understand the importance of keeping *The Rabbit Hole* a secret. After a careful discussion about what was going on in the world at large, they began to make them practice safe shooting just in case they ever had to defend themselves.

Alfi spent the time getting to know the land surrounding their property. There was a pretty healthy creek that ran through the woods, about four hundred yards from the cabin. The thing Alfi wanted to do before the winter freeze set in was to dig a root cellar, and start cutting some trees for wood. He and Sam decided to come up every weekend, and work on getting the place ready.

Work became a very surreal place for them. They got through their days, listened to their co-workers small talk about family and how crazy it had gotten. They had even allowed their children to go back to school, so the Aimeses, like every other family, struggled on. They told the children to take their cell phones everywhere they went. The adults watched and waited for news that things were improving. For a while it really did seem that things would slowly turn around. Everyone was trying to be normal. Alfi and Sam hoped for a miracle. They clutched each other at night hoping that their worst fears would not come true. But America had taken too many punches, and the people who started the decline, the bankers, their world finally collapsed. When it came crashing down, it was the end of everything. The great bright beacon to the rest of the world would go dark.

*

Chapter Three: The Collapse

"Annual income twenty pounds, annual expenditure nineteen six, result happiness. Annual income twenty pounds, annual expenditure twenty pound ought and six, result misery." Charles Dickens, David Copperfield.

Four months after the attacks, Citibank folded, then a day later Merrill Lynch, Goldman Saks. In an incredible orgy of self-immolation the banking industry collapsed. It stunned Americans and the world that in 48 hours it was all gone. With the world economy disintegrating, the big financial institutions could not call in their investments. Their world of debt was no longer sustainable. People tried going to the banks to withdraw their money. The lucky ones got some of their investments back, but most did not. Americans watched as the money they had worked hard to earn disappeared. The Cyprus Doctrine came into play. Alfred couldn't help thinking that his buddy Patrick Finnegan was right all those years ago. There was no one to hold accountable. The Aimeses were not immune. They had close to three hundred thousand in various accounts and lost about two thirds of it. Alfi had gone back and forth with himself over whether he should have bought more silver and gold, but it was too late now.

They watched as all across America, there were runs on the banks. There were even instances of violence. Several people lost their lives as disgruntled customers either tried to take their money back by force or just ran amok with knife, gun, or bat. The failure of the banks was catastrophic. It was ironic that they, the financial institutions, managed to accomplish what the terrorist couldn't. The failure brought the country to its knees. Oil prices shot up, along with food prices, and people were more concerned about their families and their money to keep the supply infrastructure in place. Alfi and Sam found themselves in a situation where there was no food in the stores, and then to make matters worse the country's infrastructure began to fail.

The effect the banking failure had on businesses was catastrophic. As businesses couldn't pay their workers, or move their products, they were forced to close their doors. With all those people now sitting home with little money and food, there was a spike in crime. At first there was a spike in domestic disputes but as the days ticked by—it was now a week after 'The Collapse'—Law enforcement began to see a gradual increase in more serious crime. The lurking dragon of those 100 million people who were on government assistance and who longer had any means of feeding themselves and their families became a dangerous issue.
*

"This is crazy," Samantha said as she replaced the phone in its receiver. "They actually want me to come into the hospital. They say that I am emergency personnel and that I could face severe charges if I don't go in." She looked at Alfi and frowned.

"Charges, what kind of charges are they talking about?"

"Well Mary, our nurse manager said that she got word that they are about to reinstitute martial law, and that hospital personnel are required to be on call." Alfi thought about this for awhile. He sat on a chair at their dinner table in the kitchen. He mentally calculated how much money they had on hand, and food and gas stored, and figured that they could stay put and hunker down for the next three months at home or more without either of them paying any bills or working. Even if they lost power they would be okay. He had enough firewood out back to keep them warm during the coming winter months, and he had power from his Sunrnr solar system to run vital appliances. He looked at his wife and said "Hell with it. Your family needs you now. We will both stay put with the kids. Everything is now at a standstill. We watch the news every day and all they can tell us is that Congress is in an emergency session with the President." He shook his head in disgust. "It's all about keeping ourselves and the kids safe now."

Alfi's boss had told all his workers to stay home while the banking crisis was going on. The yogurt factory had been affected like almost every other business. They could not ship their product, or pay their major bills. For safety reasons they decided to close the factory and pay the security guards to keep watch in case of looting. They thought that this was just a temporary thing, most people did. But Alfi did not think that the fix was going to come any time soon.

When mass riots began in New York City, Samantha realized how fragile a hold the government had on maintaining law and order. The supermarkets and food marts had been running low on food. Most had been forced to close. The people of the city stuck it out for ten days before panic finally set in. The mayor tried to calm his citizens' fears by telling them that emergency food supplies were on the way. But when day eight turned into day ten and the supplies were still not available, the dam broke. It was tragic and destructive. Over two hundred thousand people went berserk. It rippled through the city, a swarm of hungry desperate people. Any place that seemed to have food was plundered, restaurants, supermarkets, cafes, and schools. No place was safe.

The police tried to restore order but were soon overpowered, and found themselves in a fight for their lives as they were attacked. The death toll was fifteen people on the first day and rose to two hundred on the second day. Police trying to break up the riots found themselves under attack, and responded with deadly force. Business owners trying to protect their property were either killed or killed looters.

When the fires started, an already hellish scene was made even grimmer. This would set the pattern for the other food riots which then flared up around the country. Americans watched as people of every race, color and creed, young and old, conservative and liberal, rioted and killed their fellow man. There were even reports of people breaking into their neighbors' apartments because they thought they had food. It always ended with the military being called in to stop the riots. But soon they found themselves in running battles with armed or unarmed mobs. Soon cities all across the country were in flames. Ten days without food seemed to be the trigger in all cases. Samantha watched as most of the cities across the country devolved into anarchy. Neighbor turned against neighbor, families against other families.

She realized that it was just a matter of time before the madness spread their way. She wondered just how prepared they were for it. Again and again her mind went to her children. She felt a real gripping fear claw at her heart. Her family was the most important thing to her. She always knew how much she cared for Alfi and the kids, but the scenes of rioting and hungry desperate people made her flush with real anger. She knew without a doubt then that she would kill to protect her family. It was so clear and absolute that it made her actually feel better, stronger. The fear was still there but she reckoned that it was a good thing to feel that fear. It meant that she would not become complacent.

She spent that day and the following trying to reach family members. Her parents were in North Carolina and Alfi's dad lived by himself in a small house just outside of Utica, NY. Alfi's mother had died six years ago from breast cancer. Her parents insisted that they were okay and Alfi's dad insisted that he was okay, that he and his neighbors were looking out for each other.
*

On the thirteenth day of 'The Collapse' the power went out for the first time. The first blackout lasted four hours, and then the lights came back on. The second time a day later they went off and stayed off. That was when Alfi went into full survival mode. He placed all his solar lamps outside to charge. He also decided to blacken the windows, by placing ripped up black garbage bags over them so that the house attracted a lot less attention from the road during the night.

The Sunrnr system was now fully operational. After playing around with it for a few days, they finally got the hang of working with their solar backup power supply. He would plug in the refrigerator only when it began to get too warm for any meat he was storing. He did not use any electricity at night. The entire family bunked in the living room where he got a fire going in the wood stove, which kept the immediate area warm. For Candice and Robert it was both fun and frightening; it seemed that they were taking part in some grand adventure, or playing a part in some movie. The harsh reality of the situation had not yet sunk in for them.

For the first time Alfi began to keep one of the 12 gauges by the side of his sleeping bag. He would listen to the local radio station at night. He marveled at the dedication of the radio staff. Most channels were off the air. There were only a few news companies whose staff thought that reporting on the Banking Emergency, as they were still calling it, was a journalistic necessity. The local AM radio station had vowed to their listeners to continue broadcasting until it was no longer possible to do so. They were on the air 3 hours a day. First broadcast was at 8 am, the next one was at noon and the final broadcast of the day was at 8 PM.

Tonight Alfi and Sam listened, sitting in chairs by the stove. The children were already asleep in their sleeping bags. They listened to Donald Rovey as he ran through the local news:

"Martial law has now been officially declared in Broome County; no one is to venture out after 6 PM. Roads are to remain clear for emergency personnel. All essential emergency personnel are supposed to be at their stations. The local supermarkets are out of food and closed. Local farmers are being sounded out to set up a farmers' market to sell food this weekend at Otsiningo Park. The town has set up special deliveries of basic supplies that are being delivered every couple of

days to elderly people. There is no idea how long these supplies and deliveries will continue."

"The situation around Syracuse is one of utter devastation. Just like with the other nuked cities the danger area of highest contamination extends out 20 miles from the blast zone. All the communities immediately around the city have major problems. There is a mandatory evacuation order for the city itself and some the immediate surrounding areas. They are testing the water, air, and soil constantly for contamination. They don't know how much of the particles got into the atmosphere and where it ended up. The towns of Nedrow, Jamesville, Fayetteville, Minoa, Liverpool and Camillus have been told that they need to consider themselves within the immediate zone for contamination. The really frightening thing is the possible contamination of the Onondaga Watershed area, not to mention all the valuable farms around the blast zone. This is really bad folks. I would suggest for all of us here in Broome County to keep vigilant and test your water and food constantly for radiation."

"Hunters are banging away in the woods and state lands in unprecedented numbers. There has been a huge rush to validate hunting and fishing licenses. People are trying to feed their families the old fashioned way. There has been some looting and thefts of food and neighbor assaults are steadily rising. The general consensus so far is that Broome County residents are hanging on by a thread. Local law enforcement has issued an emergency edict; it gave any land owner the right to protect their property and families from any assault or theft. The police are over run."

Alfi and Samantha found themselves holding hands as they digested the new info. "The farmers' market sounds great. It would be chance to probably get some fresh vegetables," Sam remarked. She then thought about it a little more and realized that it would probably be a bad idea. "Probably a bit of risk though. Can't say how much food would be available, or what type of food would be available and how expensive it all would be. The whole county is going to be there. I have a feeling that things might get a bit desperate." Her husband nodded in the semi darkness. "Think you might be right. There are a lot of people who don't have any food left in their homes. They will be desperate. A hungry desperate mob is the worst mob. They all have children and families to feed. I can see things getting a bit problematic."

It was then Alfi decided that, starting in the morning, he would be keeping a sharper eye out. It was time to tell his wife about his plan to start keeping a roving night watch in five hour shifts. Since 'The Collapse' he had not really had a chance to chat with any of his neighbors. The Gilberts who lived at the end of Pine Road had been gone for a while. They were an older couple, and he had seen them leave in their camper about three weeks ago. They were not back yet.

The Parsons were around. He could tell they were home because he had seen smoke coming out of their chimney up to that very evening. There was farm land on a great portion of Pine Road so the neighbors were few and far between. There were four other homes on Pine. Alfi then realized that he had never really paid too much attention to those other people. He almost slapped himself then. How could he have been so blind? He resolved to learn more about the people who lived on his street. It may a bit too late but he wanted to know who they were and how they were faring. The street was two miles long from end to end. He resolved to walk it quickly in the morning, just to see what was going on. The thought of leaving Samantha and the kids alone made his stomach tighten, but he realized that it was necessary to get a view of what going on in his neck of the woods.

He then chatted with Sam about his plans. He could tell that she did not like the idea of him wandering about on his own but she understood why he needed to scout around a bit. He then suggested that while he was gone she should keep the .38 revolver and the 12 gauge handy, and watch the road and yard through the upstairs windows until he was back. As the fire burned down they made their plans for the morning.
*

It was a fine day for it. He could not help but admire the day. 'Jesus' he thought to himself, 'Mother Nature did not care a jot for what people were doing to each other.' She just moved along at her own pace oblivious or indifferent to the machinations of man. The beauty of the morning made him remember that scene from *All Quiet on the Western Front* when the main protagonist Paul Bäumer saw the butterfly, and marveled at its beauty. He smiled grimly to himself that butterfly had gotten Paul killed, its beauty had made him careless, and it was a note- to-self moment to keep his wits about him. He felt the weight of the .45 in the holster under his arm. The day, apart from being beautiful, was a crisp 38 degrees. So he was dressed warmly in a green NY Jets beanie, a heavy dark navy blue wool parka and jeans. He chose insulated ankle top hiking boots to keep his feet warm.

He decided to walk to the west end first and make his way back to the east side. His street ran in a mild downward slope from east to west. So he figured this route would be the most advantageous. The first house he came upon was the Parsons. He went up their driveway and knocked then backed away from the door. Mrs. Parsons came to the door. She was a thin graying wiry woman, with a ready smile in the best of times. She looked at him through the screen door; the smell of coffee came from the house.

"Yes Alfi, morning. How are you and Samantha?"

"We are doing as well as can be expected. I know we haven't chatted in a long while. How are you guys doing?"

"The world seemed to have gone mad," she sighed. "Any idea when things are going to get back to normal?"

"No I've been listening to the radio same as you. The internet's down. No TV now. All I know is that the government is trying to maintain some kind of order. The President's trying, but there's nothing he can do about any of this now. Best I can figure, Congress will have to find a way to get us out of this banking mess. They have got to get a quick handle on this money issue so that people can start doing business again. The only thing I can say Emily is that it's going to be a while." He paused, scratching his beard. "Is Dean alright?"

"He's alright; hurt his back moving our generator a few days ago. He'll live."

"Well if you need any help, you know where we are."

"You don't worry about it. We'll be fine," she said, and smiled.

"I'll see you both soon. Just to let you know I'm taking a walk down our street to check in on our neighbors."

"You be careful."

"I will be." He turned and walked back down their short driveway and back out to the black top of Pine Road. He heard the Parsons' screen door creak shut. The next house was just around the bend and over a rather steep hill. He had never really talked to these people before. They seemed to be a large family, a rather rich family, by the look of things. Their house stood upon six acres. There was a rather long driveway that led up to the front yard. There were five cars parked in it. He stood in front of the house and was seized by a moment of indecision.

Suddenly his resolution to actually check on the neighbors did not seem like a good idea. He looked at the house in front of him. It was not a particularly picturesque abode. It was a large house, six bedrooms, painted white and grey, and it reminded him of houses he had seen in documentaries that people with six wives built to house their large families. As he took in the Janus' house, for that was the name on the mailbox, he sensed that the home was constructed not for beauty or out of love, but for purely utilitarian purposes. He spotted a couple of four wheelers parked beside the garage. Consumerism without taste or joy.

He lost his nerve. He turned and began to walk back to his home. The joy of the day was gone; the sense of adventure and purpose was gone. He felt vulnerable, and fear, visceral and bitter, coursed through him. His breathing became short and erratic and his chest tightened as what he knew was a bad case of heart burn began to rake its claws up his throat. Why

was he so frightened? He was scared because he realized then and there that he and his family were utterly alone. In a world of every man for himself, anyone not family or friend was potentially the enemy. He realized that the Janus' house had creeped him out because he had sensed in a very primal way that they were the competition. They were a bigger family, with potentially bigger and better resources. He hurried home on that beautiful fall morning, full of doubt and terror. The less his family saw of others and the less they saw of them, the better their chances of survival.
*

When he stepped on his porch the door opened almost immediately, and Sam emerged with the .38 in her hand. She self-consciously tucked the revolver into the waist of her jeans. He could hear the children laughing about something inside. His heart was still racing but he had gotten it under control. He had made a promise to himself to never let his family see him indecisive or disheartened. He sat down in a rocking chair, while she stood and leaned up against a post. He noticed again just how beautiful she was as the sun glinted off her red hair.

"Do you think things will be okay Alfi?"

"Yeah I do. But it will not come as quickly as we are all hoping for. This mess that we got ourselves in is a real big one. It's going to take a whole lot of fixing. There are a lot of people who are anti government. Well the only thing that can get us out of this nightmare will be the government. A new government of the people by the people, for the people. If we are going to save this country, keep the Union intact and the American dream and ideals alive, then we need the leaders to figure something out. The heart of the country has been ripped out and they, well we, are going to have to repair it. The problem right now is that everyone is looking out for themselves only. There is no real sense of the collective, no sense of community. That's the scary part. It was amazing how everyone was singing Kumbaya during the first 72 hours or so, but soon after, when they realized that the problem was not going to be fixed in a short time, they began to turn on each other. There are a lot of people who believe in the goodness of man. Those people I think for the most part are going to be mighty disappointed. Random acts of kindness will be few and far between."

"The rich people have fleeced the country. I wouldn't be surprised if they are in safe havens waiting it all out. The middle class and the poor are going to have to fight it out, and save this country. That's what Americans have to really get, really understand. It's not a Conservative vs. Liberal issue, or a religious or racial issue, it's a Preserving the Union issue. The people who were supposed to guide us and protect the Union have betrayed us. We had this idea of America the land of the free, the home of the brave, and the place where if you worked hard, you should be able to provide for your family. Those things were neglected by people who only wanted to advance themselves—their ideology, greed, egos. I fear for the Union. I hope we can get this thing fixed and we can begin to repair the damage. Our generation, you and I, we are essentially done—Most people our age and older have had their entire savings wiped out, retirement plans gone. All government benefits, gone—no more Medicaid and Social Security. If things ever get back to 'normal' we are going to have to live the rest of our lives scraping together every bit of cash to be able to live in some sort of dignified way. We are poor now Samantha, we used to be middle class, and at this point there is no middle class, just poor people. The best thing to do probably would be just to live up at *The Rabbit Hole*, live off the land, fight anyone who intrudes on our property and lifestyle."

"Some people actually wanted this. But what they did not understand was that, if this thing gets as bad as I think it will be, there will be no one to protect them. There will be no law, no religion, no political ideology, and no justice. There will always be someone who will have more guns, more smarts, and more people. It's all very scary. I hope that we will get through it, hell I just want our children to survive it. That's our mission now I guess. We do what we can to make sure Candice and Robert come through at the other end of this nightmare in one piece."

Samantha looked at her husband. She looked at him in a way that she hadn't in a long time, not so much as her husband, but as a man, a fellow struggling human being and she understood. She felt sadness inside. It made her shake and sob. Alfi was about to get up and come to her but she held her hand out, begging him to stay where he was. She cried because her life that she had spent and dedicated so much energy building was essentially gone. Even if they came out of this thing alive, the world on the other side was going to be very different from the one they had lived in, and that was scary. She felt a surge of hate for the politicians, terrorists, for the mercenary companies, unethical media, and banks that had put them in the present mess. Her face was flushed and her eyes shone. It was going to take a miracle to put Humpty Dumpty together again.

*

That night after listening to the 8PM radio broadcast, Alfi began his roving watch. It took him around the perimeter of the house. He would stop at windows that gave him a great view of his yard and the tree line beyond the lawn. He would scan the woods and brush with his night vision goggles. He would move through the house to a different vantage point every ten minutes. He did his rounds with the Mini 14 under one arm. He figured that if there was an immediate threat he would be better able to respond quickly and efficiently.

He also had a digital camera in his shirt pocket. The idea had occurred to him that if someone attacked them, and if they had to respond, it would do well to be able to document the issue in some way. He kept the battery for the camera charged using a solar charger. If there was an altercation he would turn it on, put it in movie mode, and place it somewhere where it could record the action. That way if there happened to be a body or two; he would be able to explain himself to the powers that be when the time came.

When Sam's turn came to take the watch, he explained the routine. She made her rounds with a flask of hot tea, which helped to keep her alert. While doing the rounds Samantha once again had some insight as to how serious the situation had become. A year ago she would have never dreamed that she would be walking around her own home with a semi-automatic rifle, watching for people who would want to do her family harm.

She felt a wave of protectiveness for the people sleeping in the living room. It was raw and powerful. It was amazing this feeling. It was also a great clarifier.

She had been worried about her work and what might happen when they realized she wasn't going to come in. She had been feeling that she had been betraying herself and her profession. That was now completely superseded by her need to protect her family. That was the highest duty. It was her ultimate responsibility to protect the people sleeping in the living room.

   She thought about altruism. There was the idea that people who excelled or who were remembered for their public service were people who put others before themselves. They had put the good of all before their family and themselves. She wondered if she should be ashamed that she was putting her family before her duty as a nurse. But the simple fact was that if she was at work and her family was harmed in some way she would not be able to forgive herself. That made the decision of where she ought to be clear in her mind. She wondered how many other people were having the same dilemma. Family ties were strong. She also knew that there would be some people who would put themselves first before anyone else even family. There would be that father, mother or child who would run away. They would leave that husband behind, or child, parent, baby or wife. They would walk away. Some would find freedom and some would find hell in their decision.
*

Chapter Four: The Fire

The next day, around 10, when they had finished their morning meal and were cleaning up, Alfi saw someone coming up the street through the windows in the kitchen. It was a single individual, dressed in jeans and a heavy dark coat with a hood that he or she wore up over the head. He motioned to Samantha to look and they watched as the person walked slowly up the street. The person had a backpack. As the individual drew nearer, Samantha stiffened a bit and said slowly. "I think it's the Janus' girl, the older one who worked with her father at their office in Conklin." Alfi had never really paid too much attention to the people living on his street, so he took her word for it.

"Do you think we should go out and chat?" he asked. "No" Sam said. "I think that we should just keep our head down now. We should not invite anyone to chat. We should just mind our own business. Whatever the reason why she is walking away from her home on such a cold day cannot be good."

So they watched as the young woman slowly trudged her way down the road. It became a tantalizing mystery to the Aimeses as to why she would be going away from home, especially on foot after Alfi had seen all those vehicles in the driveway the day before. For some reason he remembered the chill he got standing there in front of the Janus' house and his brow furrowed in worry.

"I think you were right," he said to Samantha, "I think the policy of laying low is the policy of survival. Keeping our eyes open and staying out of sight as much as possible is the most probable way of not attracting trouble."

It was strange, Samantha thought, after the girl had disappeared around the bend. It was strange that she had gone off alone. Could she be leaving her family behind? Did they throw her out? For Sam it was a tantalizing morsel, something to give her mind a distraction, from the grim reality of her present circumstances. It wasn't long after she went by that they noticed smoke coming from the direction of the Janus' home. Alfi quickly put on his parka and grabbed his .45. It was funny how now he never went anywhere without it. He wondered if there was going to ever be a time when he would feel absolutely okay not going about armed.

"I'm going to go check it out," he said, as he tucked the pistol into his shoulder holster. "Do the watch while I am out, in case it's a distraction. I won't be gone long." He jogged up the street. The Janus' house was just an eight minute trot away. He went by the Parsons. He waved as he saw Emily and Dean stepping outside. They were obviously concerned about the smoke.

He ran up and around the corner, there was just one more turn and he would be able to see the house. But he didn't really need to see it to know what was happening. The black smoke was thick and his eyes began to sting. He could also hear the fire. It was an amazing sound to Alfred. It seemed like a great beast was loose and ripping up trees. He knew that sound was the fire devouring the house's frame. He slowed down because the smoke had gotten so thick he couldn't really see properly and he oriented himself so as not to get turned around. The wind shifted and he caught a glimpse of the house. The massive structure was in flames. In a move that he would later question, he actually ran up the driveway towards the burning home. He also noticed that the cars were moved to the side of the house and they were burning. He then stopped short. There was a sound, it was a scream.

Alfred stopped and listened, and over the roar of the flames, he heard the screaming again. He ran to the side of the house getting as close as he dared. The heat was unbelievable. He saw a window and a hand beating on it. He ran towards the window, and almost stopped in shock as a pale face, white and terrified came into view. It was a child, a boy he had seen around the neighborhood, waiting for the school bus in the mornings. He recognized the child, but did not know his name.

He took his coat off and wrapped it around his arm. His eyes were streaming water, from the smoke and heat, his lungs felt like they were rebelling in his chest. What he was not aware of was that he was actually sobbing, and shouting to the boy in the window. "Get back from the glass. I'll get you, I'll get you!" he raised his arm and was about to swing it towards the glass when there was a terrific shrieking sound of metal and wood. He did register that he had swung and had indeed broken the glass. That was when the house shivered and the roof came down.

There was glass, smoke, wood and fire, and he jumped back from the flames just in time. He was still screaming, but this time it was "No, no, nooo!" the entire first floor where the child had been was in flames

and the roof had fallen in. It would be awhile before he realized just how lucky he was not to have been killed himself. He must have blacked out for a second because he had no idea how he had ended up on his stomach, and just how instinctively his body took over. His rubbery legs began to dig into the dirt and he began to crawl away from the heat and flames. It seemed to Alfred that he had been crawling for a very long time, when it had only been about a hundred feet. The smoke began to thin and he crawled onto the street. He then heard voices, and looked up to see Emily and Dean scurrying over to help him. It was obvious that Dean's back was still out by the way he was moving. Emily reached down and helped him to his feet and they all moved away from the burning house.
*

"I saw the Janus' girl, Clara I think her name is, walking down the street. I wonder what happened." Emily said as they stood back from the flames, the destruction had them mesmerized. "Let's go," Dean said, "There is not a damn thing we can do here. What's done is done." They helped Alfred down the street. They offered for him to come in and get a drink of water and catch his breath, but he declined and shuffled down the street towards his own home. As he walked he slowly took stock of himself. His legs felt a bit better now, his stomach still felt like he would throw up, but at least he didn't have heart burn. His eyes were still stinging from the smoke that blew in dark intermittent bands in his direction. His coat was now dirty and he could see a few rips in the fabric. No doubt he would have to sew them up. He tried getting himself together as best he could before he turned into his own driveway and onto his porch where he sat down heavily.

Samantha came out and as soon as she saw him she let out a gasp. He looked dirty and shell-shocked. "I guess I look terrible," he said, seeing her distress. He told her about his little journey to the Januses. He told her about the boy, who had died right before his eyes. She listened, and a multitude of feelings ran through her. She admired him for trying to save the boy's life and she also got angry at him for putting himself in danger. She was not there to see it, but she could sense that she came very close to losing her husband, and the thought of that made her cold with fear. She did not think that she could survive the things to come if Alfred wasn't around. In her mind's eye she had a flash of her managing the kids by herself and she shuddered. "Damn it Alfred." She said in a low strained voice. "Don't ever do anything like that again. Let's get you cleaned up."

They went inside and he sat down on the toilet as she brought some water in a steel pot. She used a wash cloth to clean his face and arms. His mind went to the parka and he resolved to sew up the rips in the morning when the light was good.

Samantha cleaned the dirt and soot off her husband's face and she once again realized just how much she loved the man; it was fierce and deep. He was here, living and breathing and chatting with her. She could touch his warm skin and smell the earthy smell of him. She could see him smile that shy smile of his that most people took for mischievousness. She had almost lost him. It would have been so sudden, too; all he did was go up the street to check out where the smoke was coming from. The arbitrariness of it was galling, and pointed to the unpredictability of most things in general.

She wondered about the girl who had walked down the street. It would remain an unsolved mystery. Why did she leave? Did she start the fire? Did someone in the home start the fire? If so why? Samantha presumed that everyone in the house had been killed except for the girl they had seen. Why would someone kill their entire family? It was crazy. Then she began to wonder just how many people would be committing suicide, or who had committed suicide. She realized that a lot of people had lost everything they had because of 'The Collapse.' A lot of people had not stocked up on food, had not prepared and were now in a really bad way, and if they had families, oh God, she did not want to think about it anymore.

She wondered who was to blame for the mess they were in now. Was it the government? She had watched election after election as the idiots in Washington placed their party's loyalties and personal agendas ahead of the American people. Democrats and Republicans would torpedo each other because they were so intent on making the other party look bad. It had gotten to a point where nothing could get done. There had been a lot of opportunities that could have prevented the calamity they had found themselves in now, but the old men in Washington and their surrogates, the Governors, refused to work together.

Presidents had come and gone but they had little power themselves. The two party system had become corrupt, bought by powerful interest groups. The government had failed to protect its constitutional values and its citizens. Its job was the people first, but money and power had corrupted the very men who were elected to lead. The sufferers were now the middle class and the poor. She felt a vicious wave of

anger, towards those men in suits, those men in Washington, because she had almost lost her husband today, and a small boy got burned to death.
*

This was the Aimeses' first real interaction with the harsh realities of post Collapse life. It made Samantha reflect, as she looked around and saw all the technology in her home, which was proof of a highly evolved society, that it was a society that was in danger of going extinct. The United States of America was in danger, and it made her angry. She had never been what she might call very patriotic. But the fact that the Union was in danger, that greedy, corrupt, inept people put it there, made her blood boil.

It wasn't until the next day that the fire finally burned itself out. There was no response from the fire department, and in all sense of the word it no longer existed. It was a lesson to the Aimeses that they were truly on their own. His experience with the fire made Alfred take a closer look at their ability to fight a fire if it did happen. He had bought two extinguishers, one for the upstairs and one for the downstairs, but if they were attacked and someone tried to burn the house, he realized that they would be almost defenseless. He realized that he had overlooked this possibility, and he chastised himself for the oversight. He did not know how to solve the problem and it began to drive him crazy. He kept seeing the face of the boy, and the face would morph into either Candice or Robert.

Finally he came up with what even he thought was a wacky solution. He had a 100 foot hose that he kept in the shed. He went out and got it and moved it into the first floor pantry. The plan was if someone did try to burn them out they could run the hose from the kitchen sink to either the front porch, back deck or through the two upstairs skylights. The solution was wholly inadequate but it made him feel better. He then realized just how overlooked the possibility of having to fight a fire, either when you came under attack or after an attack, was in most of the prepper/survivalist literature he had read. If worst came to worst, he and Samantha were now prepared to leave the house in a real hurry, even under fire.

They spent the next couple of days drilling the evacuation of the house in an emergency, grabbing their bug out bags, their guns, and certain important documents. They went through it a couple of times until they and the children knew what to do. If there was a firefight the kids would be moved to the safest part of the house, the bathroom, where they would lay down in the old fashioned iron tub until their parents were able to get them. They had finally fully awakened to the harsh reality of their new world, and their resolve would soon be tested.

*

"Hello folks this is Donald Rovey the time now is 8 PM. I hope you are all keeping it together out there in the Twin Tiers. It's been a testing time for all of us across the country. I hope you are not wasting any valuable battery power listening to this broadcast that you will need to light your homes tonight. The news is grim. I know that some people, believe it or not, are still working. If you are in the military, you are on duty, and if you are in the police force, the health and emergency professions, you are still working. If you are a local government representative, you are still working. If you are an old codger like me you are still working."

"Ehhem, let me just get a glass of water here, water from the Susquehanna river, filtered of course. If you have listened to my show over the years you know that my sweet Frieda passed away four years ago, my children are grown and they live in another part of the country. That's why I am still here ladies and gentlemen. This is not the time for lies or hypocrisy anymore. If my wife was still alive I would not be here broadcasting. Not in these times when people are killing each other over a scrap of bread. Not when babies are now starving, because their parents have nothing to give them and there is no help conceivably in sight."

"If I was still a family man I would have to be with my family now. I would be afraid to have left them alone, in these dark times. The way I am collecting the news is also very interesting. I walk about the streets of the city and I ask the people I see questions. The still well fed military, at their various check points, sometimes answer my questions and when I take a jaunt up to the hospital, I see what's happening. I also am an old ham and I get a lot of my info from other hams in other cities, and I scan the emergency bands to see if there is anything new. Now here is what I have been told and what I have seen."

'The farmers' market over the weekend was in all sense of the word a disaster. There was not enough produce to go around. I was there at Otsiningo Park. There were just thousands of people, families with crying children and even people who had come from out of town. They tried to distribute the food in an orderly way but there were not enough soldiers for the crowd. The farmers had brought a lot of food but it still wasn't enough. They should have figured that it was never going to be enough. It got ugly when it became clear *after awhile that the food wasn't going to be enough for everyone. It's hard to see fellow Americans starving. It was a sight to see people of every color and creed all united in their pain and suffering."*

"They tried to do the right thing, give the folks with families food first. But hunger is a heartless task master; it turns the best into madmen. Good Americans, starving Americans cried out because the food was almost gone, and they lashed out at the providers, and the soldiers. It was bad dear listeners. I personally saw fourteen people die when they were shot down by the soldiers who were then fighting for their lives. I saw two men and a woman corner a soldier and beat him to death with rocks and sticks."

"Some of the farmers who had responded as humanitarians were beaten and killed. It was a bad day for the Southern Tier; it was a bad day for Americans. If they do have another food drive you can bet the security will be a lot tighter. It was one of the saddest events I have ever covered as a newsman."

"It took a couple of hours to check out what's going on at the local hospitals. I can tell you that Binghamton General is for all sense and purposes closed, but Wilson Hospital is open. The government is trying to keep it and Lourdes Hospital operational. They are running a skeleton staff. Most of the workers have opted to stay with their families and I can tell you that they are only taking the most serious trauma cases."

"I also want to say that I have been hearing some really disheartening news about the treatment of the Syracuse Nuke Survivors. I know that they were initially transported to hospitals in the surrounding areas. I have also learned that while most died there were many that survived and are horribly disfigured. Just imagine losing

your home and maybe your family and now you are mutilated and possibly going to die within a few months or a year because of your exposure. And now you have to deal with this post collapse nightmare world. My heart goes out to these people."

"When I managed to speak with the local police, I was told that homicides in our city of Binghamton and surrounding areas have skyrocketed. I was warned to avoid any suspicious large crowds as some people have banded together to find food, and they don't care how they get it. There have been countless instances of looting and armed robberies. So this is for all you listeners out there be careful, there are people out there who will attack you if they think you have any food, or anything they can steal to trade."

"I heard it on the ham that the government was still trying to do something to get us out of this mess. The problem is that they have got what I am going to start calling a rampaging situation on their hands. As it stands right now they have no way of getting the situation back under control. Maybe if it was just the collapse of the banking system they could have dealt with that. But those nuclear strikes have compounded the situation. From what I heard the cities that were attacked are now uninhabitable. There is a twenty mile no go zone around the cities because of all the fallen ash and the threat of radioactive particles present in the air and water."

"People had been harping on this economic problem for years, and we had always seemed to find a way to handle the debt, but this attack was the final push that sent us over the edge. The terrorists struck a mighty blow for their cause and we annihilated their cities. Every country now has its own problems. The

banking industry for all intents and purposes is now defunct. It will take some time to reintroduce a monetary system that people can trust. All the major American cities are now basically war zones. People are banding together to fight and protect their property and their families. The Hungry have formed their own gangs to take from the people who have. Even here in Binghamton, the gangs are killing and burning houses to take whatever food and supplies they can steal."

"In all cities there is no electricity, water, or basic services. I don't think it will be long before disease raises its angry head, as people are disposing of their waste and sewage where they eat and sleep. Word to the wise, keep yourself as clean as possible and if you are eating make sure that your hands and the food or water are safe."

"There are desperate people out there, there are opportunists out there, there are selfish people out there, and there are good people out there. Protect your loved ones and yourselves. This is Donald Rovey, until next time."

*

Chapter Five: Looters

Samantha was up and doing her rounds while the children were blissfully asleep. It was 6:30 AM, and the cold sun was hidden by the heavy, dirty grey clouds that hung over their neighborhood. She stood scanning the yard through the living room window, when she saw something that made her smile. It had begun to snow. Big heavy flakes drifted down from the sky. It was early November, and this seemed like it was going to be the first really substantial snow shower of the season. They had gotten a little rain and some short flurries but nothing that stuck. The winter had seemed to be going the way of winters lately in the Twin Tiers, mild and unseasonably warm. It seemed like global warming was winning the day.

As the snow became thicker, she was filled with a solemn regret for the winters past, when everyone was shopping and cheesy Christmas music blared everywhere. The wind began to pick up and the snow came faster, cutting down visibility to really just a few feet. She realized that if this was a normal day, the kids would most likely be staying home, a snow day. In an hour or so there would have been snow plows and salters going about their business. The children would have gone out and played in it for a while. Before the work of shoveling the driveway had to be done, they would have all gone onto the porch and admired the beauty of the snow covered landscape all around them.

She wondered if her children would ever have those moments, of good times, or if their world would now be one of struggle and strife. Once again she felt angry at the people who allowed it all to happen. She had had this conversation with Alfred, and he said that at the heart of it all every American was to blame. They voted in candidates whose agendas were to protect certain people, and to push certain dogmas. These men and women had carved up the country so that their own parties could win elections ignoring the voice of the people. The will of the majority, the voice of the middle class was ignored and the poor were crushed. The rich got richer and they snickered and called it the American Way, free enterprise as they plundered the wealth of the country. She remembered a time when the government was in a constant case of grid lock, when one party or the other would refuse to work with the other. They had thought that if they compromised they would be thought weak.

She had always hated the two party system. There was no middle ground. She had always hoped for a party that would have provided a viable central option. The problem as she saw it was that because the two major parties were so far apart on most of the important issues, there was always gridlock in the running of the government. There was not a party that gave voters a more central option, a party that would have been able to get things moving in Washington. It would have been the bridge between the two extreme poles. Its members would have allowed bills that needed to pass to pass and prevented the gridlock that eventually suffocated the country.

She remembered the *fracking* debate that had gone on in NY. She remembered how the politicians had delayed and delayed and then allowed it, for votes and money. She remembered how the companies had moved in with their trucks and had drilled. The rich land owners then moved away. The ones who stayed were poor but still had to buy or have fancy filtration systems set up in their homes. She remembered the shock of New York City residents when they realized that their water sources had a high probability of being compromised. She remembered the conversations she had with Alfred about how all the laws were now slanted in the interests of big business and how the country was slowly killing or rather strangling the citizens who lived in it. Every single big business corporation basically lied to the public with the governments' help, she realized. The politicians were all corrupt and the media lied, they all had chosen up sides and no one told the truth, just their truth. The Constitution was basically shredded. She realized that for a long time the country was slowly taking away its citizens rights, while the air, water, food, and rights under The Constitution were being destroyed. 'Well' she thought, 'I guess the *idea* could have only lasted so long before human frailties took over. Heck even Rome fell didn't it?'

She grimaced remembering the utter arrogance of the politicians who showed in the end that they had not really cared for the common people. They were more interested in taking care of their own self interests. She now felt utter desolation, because it was these same people who were supposed to bring the country back from the brink of complete and utter ruin.

Her reverie was interrupted by a loud concussive sound. She went into the living room to wake Alfi and saw that he was already getting to his feet. The children were asleep. "Did you hear that?" He rubbed his eyes and slipped the .45 into its holster. She shook her head and noticed that her breathing was coming very fast. It was as if somehow they knew that something was very,

very wrong. That sound was not a normal sound on Pine Road. It was a sound from other parts of the world where war roamed the streets. Once again Alfi found himself going on a scouting mission. He slipped into his boots, kissed Sam and said softly. "I have to check it out"

*

He slipped out the side door and walked up the street in the direction of the Parsons' house. He pulled up short and a harsh hiss escaped through his teeth. The snow was still coming down and there was about an inch of it on the ground. His hand went immediately to the butt of the .45. Someone had rammed a truck through the Parsons' front wall. The whole front of the house had been demolished by the vehicle. His skin turned to ice as he heard the unmistakable sound of gunfire coming from within the residence. His first reaction was to run to help his neighbors, but he checked himself and ran to the side of the road and hid in the woods to watch. He saw as two tall beefy men and a thin rat-like woman came out of the residence. They were hauling large canvas bags of stuff out of the Parsons' home and throwing them into the back of the truck.

The truck itself was a beast. It was a 4-door Dodge Ram, black with silver chrome. There was a huge heavy pointed steel grille on the front of it. The use of said grille was now very apparent. They had used it to ram through the sheet rock and wood of the older couples' wall. They backed the truck out of the gaping hole, and gunning the engine they roared off down the street, in the opposite direction away from Alfred's house. He stood transfixed to the spot for a while, barely breathing, and a feeling of dread coursing through him.

Then his feet began to move. He broke cover and walked towards the house. There was still smoke and the smell of gunpowder was in the air. The damage to the building was devastating. The truck had rammed clean through the wall into the kitchen. It had destroyed the beams that held up the front part of the roof, which was now sagging dangerously.

He put his hands over his nose and squinted against the heavy dust that still swirled around inside the one story ranch. Walking through the wrecked house he came upon the first body. Dean was lying on his back in the corridor that went from the front door to the living room. He was staring sightlessly up at the ceiling. A big red ragged hole in his chest told Alfred all he wanted to know. He then went around the living room to the other side of the house. There he found Emily on her stomach in one hand she was clutching some plastic that Alfred recognized as coming from a bag of Idaho potatoes. As he looked around the pantry he realized that a fight must have taken place, and Emily paid the ultimate price. There was nothing of real value left in the pantry.

Somewhere in the back of his mind he knew that really desperate looters would have taken what they could have found, and killed the owners; this was the way things were now. He was repulsed by the violence. He became angry; these people didn't deserve to die the way they did. They were regular Americans who played by the rules all their lives. This was what it looked like when the government failed its people. A cold anger flooded through him. He decided that he would make sure that no one would get anything from the scraps left behind. Finding some matches in the kitchen he lit the curtains and waited until the fire caught in the kitchen, and the carpet and walls began to burn. He said a silent goodbye to his neighbors and realized in his heart that he was saying goodbye to his previous life. He went across the street and watched as the house began to burn. When the heat got too much he trudged through the snow back home.

*

He told Samantha everything. He realized that it was too late to drop some massive stones in his yard to protect the house. But he had a feeling that the *Truck Gang*, as he began to call them, would be back. They were not going to find his home an easy target. He wracked his brain with a way to stop that truck and decided that some Molotov cocktails would probably do the trick. He got six liquor bottles from his cabinet and filled them with gasoline then re-corked them. Then he soaked some cloth strips in gasoline and tied them around the top of the bottles. If they came at his house he would get on his porch and light them up. He got two lighters and showed Samantha how to toss the bombs.

*

During the next few nights they kept watch together. One usually kept an eye on the front and the other at the back of the house. Instead of sleeping in the living room, the children slept in the corridor outside the bathroom now. They had drilled the kids on how to get into the tub once they heard Mom or Dad shout, "Get down! Get down!", or heard real gunfire. Both the kids wanted to help, but neither he nor Sam wanted them to be exposed to danger. Two nights after the Parsons' attack, Alfred standing at his post looking out the kitchen window saw a big vehicle pull up at the corner of the road about 500 yards from his house. He looked at his watch and saw it was 5 AM. Everything became crystal clear in his mind. He knew that he was seeing the same truck and they would soon attack his house. Knowing that he only had a few minutes, he shouted to his wife and herded the kids into the bathroom. They got into the tub, and he placed a .38 in Robert's hands.

He and Samantha ran to the front door, popped it open and slid quietly into the darkness on the porch. "You really think it's them?"

"I would bet the house on it." They crouched on the porch in the darkness watching the vehicle's headlights. Their eyes were getting used to the darkness and Alfred reached down and gave her one of the crude incendiary devices. "When they come they will try the same thing they did at the Parsons. They will be thinking that they are taking us by surprise and will try to ram that truck into our house. When they attacked the Parsons there were three of them. I think there will be more this time. I think that they will have convinced a few more people to join them in their 'hunting and gathering' scheme. Well when the bastards come down our road and when they turn off to drive that thing into our yard, bend down behind the hedge, light two of these little mamas and toss them at the truck's windshield. Then immediately fire at it. Aim for the windshield. Then depending on how things go we shoot at anything that moves." Sam nodded in the darkness, and unlike her husband there were no butterflies in her stomach. She was shocked to discover that she was angry and that she wanted to hurt the people who were going to threaten her family. Alfred had a 12 gauge tactical Mossberg in his hands loaded interchangeably with pellets and slugs. The Mini 14 was across his back. There were six shells in the pump action.

The truck rolled silently down the street and when it was about two hundred feet from the house it turned sharply and revved its engine. Sounding like a beast in Hell it thundered towards the house. Samantha knew she only had seconds to act. Bending down she flicked her lighter and lit the wicks of two Molotovs. Alfred did the same and then they threw them at the oncoming truck.

The bombs were a lot more spectacular and effective than anything Alfred had imagined. Three of the incendiaries exploded and burst into flames on the windshield and the hood. The other one exploded in the truck's bed and two men leaped over the side to avoid the sudden flames. As Alfred reached down to light and throw the last two, the truck swerved and clipped an old pine tree. He heard the quick 'pop, pop, pop!' of Samantha's Mini 14 and the smashing of glass as he threw the last two cocktails.

The truck looked like something out of a nightmare. On fire, it swerved around on their lawn. The driver was still trying to orient it to run it into the side of the house, but the flames were making it impossible for him to see properly out of the windscreen. A small part of Alfred's brain was awed that the little petrol bombs were so effective. He aimed the 12 gauge at the windshield and pulled the trigger. The glass disintegrated. He worked the pump again and this time he aimed for the truck's driver window. The big hulking machine suddenly slowed, but it did not stop as it missed the side of the house and rolled across his backyard smashing into an old Douglas fir tree.

He heard the buzzing of bullets as they went by him and he turned his attention to the two men that had jumped from the back of the truck. They were now hiding behind his shed and were firing at them. He beckoned to Samantha and told her swiftly what he meant to do. Quickly and silently he slipped into the house and out the back door on the other side as Sam kept them busy. He glided noiselessly into the woods surrounding his house and made his way carefully to the back of his shed. He could see the two men firing at his wife on the porch. They were so focused on returning fire they did not see or hear him. Leaning the pump action against a tree he took aim with the light Mini 14 and squeezed the trigger twice. One attacker fell forward; and the other shouted and began to turn. He shot him twice.

Samantha saw as her husband took out the two behind the shed. She scanned the truck that was now burning and realized that it must surely explode and it did. "PAARRUMMMPPPHHH" the vehicle's gas tank blew and the truck disintegrated, sending shrapnel flying in all directions. It became a spectacular fire ball, casting the yard and house in a hellish bright yellow glow. Sam's ears were ringing from the blast and she realized that she could hardly hear anything. She saw her husband melt back into the trees and knew that he was going to go back the way he came. If Alfred was anything, he was careful and slightly neurotic.

She smiled and turned to the front door with the intention of seeing to the kids. Robert was at the door. He pushed it open and looked out warily. Samantha was about to tell him to get back inside when she felt an intense burning in her left shoulder. She saw his eyes go big and round, and he shoved her out of the way, pulling the trigger on the .38 four times. Robert was not as big as Alfred, but he was strong and he was frightened when he shoved her. She spun around and landed on her butt.

She saw her son shoot and looked in the direction he was aiming. She saw what must have been one of the men from the truck hiding behind a tree and shooting back. In an instant a fear so sharp made her scream for her son. It was true; things seemed to slow agonizingly down. She saw the bullets striking the walls and one smashed in one of the glass windows on the front of the house. She brought the Mini up and although her left arm felt like putty, she aimed for the shadowy figure and squeezed the trigger rapidly. She saw the man fall backwards and saw his body jerk as another bullet struck home.

She kept her eye on him for a while to make sure he wasn't moving. She then glanced at her son who looked at her, ashen-faced. She could see his mouth moving, could not hear what he was saying, but it needed no explanation. She reached for him and pulled him into her chest. The world sped up again to normal speed, and she could just make out he was saying "Mom, Mom, Mom," over and over again. He was crying.

She made herself let go of her son and she walked over to the body of the man who almost killed her. In the flickering light of the burning truck she could see that he was shot twice, through the upper torso and the right temple. She heard the crunching of boots and spun around, ducking, but it was only Alfred. She saw his brows contract in concern when he saw her arm. He took the rifle from her and led her back into the house. He was certain that the threat was nullified. He had inspected the bodies of attackers and had confirmed that they were all dead.

She sat down at the kitchen table and Alfred helped her out of her flak jacket and shirt. She watched as he inspected her arm. There was a large gaping wound at the top of her right shoulder. It appeared that the bullet had passed through the shoulder, ripping away a chunk of flesh in the process. Alfred got out the first aid kit and after cleaning the wound he stitched her up. He tried to be as careful and tender as he could but it was still painful. It was then they realized that with all their extensive planning, they had forgotten to get some good local anesthetic. He gave her some Ibuprofen and after swallowing them, he let her lay down for what should have been a few minutes, but the next time she would open her eyes it would be late afternoon.

*

Alfred had let the kids watch him work on their mother. He figured that one day they might need to do the same thing for him. He was proud and angry at Robert for not following the plan, but from what he heard if the boy hadn't been there to distract the attacker, Sam would probably be dead.

He looked as his son stood by the window in the kitchen scanning the yard. A feeling of remorse struck him. Sam was sleeping in the living room by the fire; Candice was watching the back from upstairs. He decided to keep a vigilant watch because he did not know if the sound of the fighting would have drawn other people to the house to investigate or loot. He decided not to take any chances. "Hey Rob, are you okay?" His voice was low. "Yeah, the fire is dying down now," the young man replied. He walked over and squeezed his son's shoulder, and realized that he was fighting back tears. A feeling of heavy gloom hung about him like a blanket.

Why was that? They had beaten the bad guys early this morning and had won. They were all still standing. They had taken out a formidable threat to their home, and lives. There was no doubt in his mind that those people would not have allowed any of them to live. He poured himself some tea and sat at the kitchen table. He realized that he had almost lost his wife and son today. The terror, the bad dreams had found him at last. He understood that their lives were now irrevocably altered. There was no going back. They had all been under fire; he and Sam had killed six people. His son had exchanged gunfire with an animal that was trying to kill him and his mother. He thought about how long they had gone without having to fight or interact with others who would be trying to take what they had. 'The Collapse' had now personally touched them all. He realized that he would have to be even more vigilant as people became more desperate. He sighed. Now was the time to go to *The Rabbit Hole*.
*

Chapter Six: Bugging Out

There were a few things that needed to be done first. He and Samantha decided that the bodies of the looters would have to be removed from the property. He placed them on a large tarp and drove them up the road to the Parsons' house. He then attached the burnt-out shell of the Dodge to the Tahoe and pulled it up there as well. Their consensus was if there was a time when they could come back home, and if there was a reestablishment of law and order, they did not want to explain the bodies in their yard. They figured that within a couple of months the burnt evidence in the yard would be covered by grass and weeds and eventually would disappear with time. It would just seem that something really bad went down at the Parsons.

They decided to wait a few days to make sure that Samantha was okay. They also needed the time to make some final arrangements before leaving their home. He and Robert went into the woods behind the house and buried caches of things they would like to retrieve if they had a chance to return. They carefully packed the Tahoe with items they deemed absolutely necessary. It was going to be very difficult to leave their home, but they all understood that the next time someone attacked them here they might not be as fortunate.

The afternoon before they left, Samantha, who luckily showed no adverse effects of her injury, spoke softly to them. "We are blessed that we are all still here. I agree that we cannot push our luck here anymore. It is clear that this thing will not be over any time soon. The government has lost control and it will take time to get things back in hand…well if they ever do. I love this

home, you guys grew up here." She looked at the kids and smiled sadly. "But now we have to leave it. This is the part that you didn't see in the books and shows about bugging out. There is a real pain leaving behind our home. You can't help wondering who will break in. Who will walk through this house and sleep here while we are gone. Will any of this still be here when it is all over? We have some wonderful memories of this house, the Christmases, the parties and dinners with friends and family. But I guess the most important thing is that we can somehow get through this and be here to help rebuild our country." Robert got up and embraced his mom. Candice did the same. Alfred got up and hugged them all. He looked at his family and once again that burning feeling of protectiveness coursed through him. He knew just how much these people meant to him and he would do anything to ensure their survival.
*

That night they tuned in to Donald Rovey again. Miracle upon miracle the old boy was still on the air. "*Hello once again dear listeners from downtown Binghamton, New York. Lots to chat about tonight so let's get started. The city is burning folks. Lots of homes have been set on fire. Best I can tell some of it is arson. People have been fighting each other over food. Bodies are in the streets. There is really no social net left. At this point it's every man, woman and child for themselves. I have been told by some buddies on ham radio that the big cities, New York, Chicago, Baltimore and the like, are under tight martial law. The government has sent in the National Guard to these and other big cities to keep the peace. But how do you keep the peace with no food folks?*"

"It has been told to me that the National Guard is under siege. They are being fought by gangs and militias. There is no trust between the people and their government anymore. Nor the people and what's left of the military. Most of the military have now left their stations and have gone to take care of their families. I have been told that New York City is hit really hard. The Guard is not allowing anyone to leave. All those New Yorkers have no weapons; they are helpless against the soldiers keeping them penned in the city. They are not allowing anyone to move in or out of the big cities period. From what I have heard there is massive starvation and it's beginning to get really ugly. There have been rumors of cannibalism."

" They want to keep the people in the big cities from leaving because they realize that it will cause a massive problem as these hungry folks will cause enormous destruction to the outlying towns, as well as the possibility of spreading disease. It's really bad in the big cities folks; remember too that most of the big cities had stringent gun laws on the books. Those people now have no way of defending themselves against each other or the people now holding them, well, should I say the word, prisoner. It's hard to look at a starving child, a dead loved one, and trust that the government will do right by the people anymore."

"There are all kinds of crazy, crazy conspiracy theories out there now. Some folks believe that this was all planned by the government as a means of gaining even more control. Some people think that this was all engineered by China and enemies of the US. Some people said that the banks were in collusion with terrorists to bring about the end of the Constitution. Whatever the answer might be, listeners, I can tell you *that no country has gotten out of this clean. This is a worldwide economic collapse. It will take us sometime to get to grips with it, and in that time many will die and are dying."*

"The one thing that gives me hope is the fact that, as bad as this thing is, most of the basic infrastructure is still in place. It hasn't been a scenario in which the world as we know is completely destroyed. My advice, listeners, is to hunker down, and see if you can outlast the chaos."

*

The following morning the Tahoe was finished being loaded and a small trailer was attached to the back. Everyone was armed. Alfi ran them through some possible scenarios. They locked up the house and said good bye to their home of seventeen years. There were two routes to their bug out location. Alfi chose the quickest and most direct. Despite the chill of the day they had the windows cracked. Each person had a firearm that they kept down and out of sight. The kids were in the back, and Samantha was driving with Alfi in the front passenger seat. As they drove away from their home, Alfi began to run through possible problem scenarios in his mind. He was hoping that the National Guard thing was only going on in the big cities. He did not want to get stopped or shuttled to some camp or other.

They got onto Barrow Road and turned left onto Jenkins Road. The Interstate was up ahead. They needed to get onto to I81 S towards Whitney Point. There was a sense of unease in the vehicle; no one had slept well the night before. There was also sense of being exposed, and vulnerable. As they got halfway up Jenkins they ran into traffic. People were in their cars honking at each other. Samantha pulled in slowly behind the last car. The road curved out of sight to the left, so it was impossible to see what was going on a mere twenty cars ahead. They rolled a few more feet and then everything came to a stop. They sat and waited for a long time. "It's been about twenty minutes," Robert said from the back seat.

"I wonder what this is all about now." Samantha sighed as she reached over to hold Alfred's hand. "Don't know and don't like it," Alfred said his chest in a knot of tension. He looked in the rear view mirror and noticed that two other cars had now pulled in behind them. The cars were now practically at a standstill. He noticed two people had gotten out of their cars and were now walking up towards the curve; this little excursion seemed to have piqued the curiosity of the other drivers as some other people left their cars to see what the holdup was about. It went through Alfred's mind that this was a lot of people here on this cold wintry morning. Gas was not available. So either they must have hoarded or somehow siphoned off a few gallons to travel. Sitting and idling your vehicle was not the thing to do now, you wanted to be on the move getting where you wanted to be, not wasting gas. "You better switch off the car while we wait," he said. Then a sudden thought hit him, and he had a burning desire to see what was going on up ahead. "I'm going to hop out and take a look."

"No Dad that sounds like a bad idea," Candice's voice had a slight edge of panic to it.

"Well it's best I see and know how to plan if there is a problem. I'll be back in a jiffy." He hopped out and jogged up the street, got to the curve and went around. There were at least twenty other vehicles in line, and further ahead he saw the National Guard trucks. There was also a small group of people who had gotten curious and were now standing in a small huddle off to the side. He walked over and joined them. "Good morning. Any idea what the holdup is?" They all turned and looked at him. Suddenly he felt like he was the idiot in the room. A tall grey haired older man wearing a ball cap, grey jacket and jeans leaned in and said quietly: "Well I heard that they were doing this, but I didn't want to believe it." Alfred looked at the other people and a frown creased his face. "What are you talking about?" he asked. A woman wearing a badly fitting cream colored beanie explained: "Well you see those soldiers up there taking all that stuff out of that car and putting it in the pile near the trucks. Well what they are doing is confiscating anything they think the army might need in the name of national security."

Alfred's face got even tighter as he quickly processed the information the woman gave him. These were National Guardsmen. The fact that they were seizing people's belongings sent all the alarm bells going. "Is this some kind of military order coming down that they need supplies?"

"Not as far as I can figure", said the last guy in the group. He was young and only wearing a thin green sweater and jeans. "I have not heard anything on the radio. It just looks like outright theft to me." Alfred didn't say anything, but that's what it started to look like to him as well. He had a lot of things in his Tahoe and the trailer. Those were his family's things. He did not want to turn them over to some guy in green. Something then caught his attention. There was a man in a black suit who was directing the Guardsmen as to what to take. As Alfred looked at him closer he came to recognize the man as Agent Lambert, the same man who had come to his house a few years ago to check up on him, from the NSA. This was all bad, and his mouth got suddenly a little dry.

He turned quickly on his heel and got back to his vehicle. His heart was thumping as his brain raced to come up with a plan. Samantha noticed his aggravation right off and asked what he had seen. He looked at her, craned his neck to look at the back of the line. There was a green military vehicle parked about five cars back. He realized to his horror that they were boxed in. There were thick woods to the left. He knew the area pretty well; he had gone hunting in them in better times. He made a decision and he knew Sam would not like it one bit, but it would give them a chance.

He turned to her with the hard expression she had come to know well, and a lump formed in her throat. "Up ahead they are taking stuff away from people. I even heard that they may siphon off the gas in the vehicles. Here's what I am going to do. I am going to walk into the woods over there and pretend that I am just taking a pee. I'll work my way around to the Guardsmen truck in the rear there. When you hear the shooting, you make the quickest K-Turn you can and drive like hell. Use the other route we had looked at before. It's longer and there are more rural roads to deal with but you should get to *The Rabbit Hole* safely. I will join you there as soon as I can. I am going to walk so it will probably take me a day or so." He looked around the Tahoe's cabin at his kids and wife, and realized that this might be the last time he sees them.

So many things could and would go wrong, he thought. Samantha was shaking her head. "We could just let them have it all and walk away." He shook his head in the negative. He knew in his bones what the deal was here. "Make no mistake about what these guys are doing. The way I figure it, and the sneaky way they have gone about what they are doing, I think that either they will not leave anyone alive, since they have snuck their truck back there in the rear. Or they are here to take what they can and then move the people into camps. I don't think we would survive in a camp where the guards have to steal to provide for themselves." He looked at his family in the car and they knew he was right. Something smelled really bad here. For the second time in a couple of days they would have to resort to extreme violence to prevent others from doing them harm.

"Okay," Samantha turned and looked at the kids in the back. "Roll down the windows. Robert use the shotgun. Now when your Dad starts shooting that's when we turn and try to make it through. We are going to have to go through the line of fire. It would have been nice if there were woods on both sides of the road, then you could have gone over on the left instead of having to do it on the right. Those suitcases there shove them up against your door Robert. I don't know what type of weapons they have but sometimes bullets can pass through car doors like tissue paper. Keep your head down and as we pass just pop the gun up and keep pumping and squeezing the trigger. I will just duck and floor it."

She felt her heart speed up and there was a cold detachment from reality. Alfred reached over and squeezed her hand. Then he kissed her long and soft, tasting her, smelling her breath. "I love you." He smiled and reached out and grabbed the kids' shoulders and squeezed. "You take care of your mother. I'll see you in a couple of days."

With that he quickly checked the clip of his trusty Colt .45 1911 model pistol. He had three extra clips attached to the shoulder holster. He took a deep breath, gritted his teeth and stepped out onto the pavement. Walking as nonchalantly as he could he went off the road a bit into the tree line across from the parked guards' truck. There were two men in the cab. They were talking animatedly, which was good for Alfred because it means that they were distracted. He needed all the edge he could get.

He would have to aim and try and get at least one with the first two shots. That would take a tricky tense moment to aim the weapon without catching their attention. He fiddled around with his pants and with his back to the two men; he removed the gun from the holster. 'This is the point of no return Alfred!' This was going to be bad killing Guardsmen, and every fiber in his being revolted at the fact of shooting men wearing the US uniform. But they were going to kill his family; he knew that in his bones. If they didn't do it here on the side of the road they would do it in a camp somewhere. He could not bear to watch his family slowly starve to death in some hellhole. That put the final steel into his resolve. He walked a little into the bushes, dropped onto one knee and fired. He saw the guard sitting on his side of the road jerk and slump forward. The other guard tried bringing up his weapon, Alfred beat him to it, he fired and saw the man hold his shoulder and drop down in the cab. He heard the screech of wheels and saw the Tahoe ripping down the blacktop. The guard shoved his M16 into the window and opened fire. Most of the bullets seemed to have passed over the top of the Tahoe but heard as some found their mark in the side of the vehicle.

As it sped by, he also heard the answering bangs of Robert working the shotgun. The pellets smashed the passenger window of the truck and forced the guard to duck. He was aware of the SUV clearing the gap at the back of the line. Then he felt a burn in his hip. He dropped flat on the ground and hugged the dirt as bullets thudded into the bushes and earth around him. He heard the guards' gun click on empty, then he made an instant decision. Run, not shoot back. As he got up to sprint, he heard more gunfire coming from further up the street. "I guess some of the other folks had made the same decision." He said grimly as he zigzagged into the woods. His hip hurt like hell but he could not think about the pain at present. He just wanted to get as far away from what would be certain carnage on the road. He dropped into a painful jog for about 20 minutes before he had to stop.

He collapsed in a heap at the foot of a maple tree. He leaned up against it and he could feel himself about to black out. He pinched himself on the arm and the pain jolted him back into crystal clear reality. He looked down on his right side and saw that he was bleeding. 'Ohh crap!' It didn't look good. He unbuckled his belt and slipped his jeans down and saw that he had a hole at the top of the thigh. He felt around back and realized that it had passed through, without hitting the bone. He leaned against the tree with relief. He felt as though he would cry. He was shot but it had gone clean through. If it had hit bone he would really have been screwed. After the initial relief he saw that he was still bleeding. Panic began squirming its way into his mind again as he realized that he had to find some way of stopping the bleeding.

He ripped off a part of his white undershirt. Then he ripped it further into strips to tie them around the wound, hoping that it would clot. Then his eye caught something, a yellow root bush. Despite the coldness of the winter it still had some leaves on it. He remembered reading somewhere that the roots contained a natural antibiotic, and that it could be an anticoagulant. He weighed the choices, infection vs. blood not clotting. He decided to take a chance on the wound not clotting for awhile to fight any infection. 'Well it can't hurt.' He said to himself as he pulled it up out of the ground.

He bit off a small piece of the root, and almost vomited. It tasted like ass. He chewed it up and then placed the masticated pieces over the two holes. He then used the strips to tie the wadding unto the wounds. He gingerly pulled his pants up, then thought about it for a second, and bit off a bit more of the root, intending to chew and swallow it. In some part of his brain he was hoping that he hadn't chewed too much and that it wasn't toxic. It was weird but he felt better.

He decided to get moving. There was a small compass in the band of his watch and he used it to orient himself. In the car the trip to *The Rabbit Hole* would have taken about an hour and a half. By foot over rough terrain, staying away from the main roads, it would take at least a day. And that was if he could keep moving steadily. He knew the biggest test would come tonight. The temperature would drop like a rock, into the low 30's. He was hungry, thirsty, and had lost some blood. As he hobbled off, he wondered if he would ever see his family again.

*

Chapter Seven: Complications

"*Anything that can go wrong, will go wrong.*" Murphy's Law

Samantha laid as low as she could and floored the accelerator. The Tahoe lurched and bucked but picked up speed. She heard Robert's shotgun going off and heard a few bullets thud into the car as she sped by the military truck. She kept her head up just enough to make sure she was steering correctly, and then before she knew it they were a mile away. Her heart was ramming in her chest and she realized that for some reason she had been holding her breath. She sat up and forced herself to breathe deeply as she kept the accelerator down. She felt like she really needed to pee as she kept looking into the rearview mirror. Surely they would send someone after her? After four, then six miles of no signs of pursuit she finally let her foot relax off the gas. She glanced at her watch. The whole thing from when Alfred started shooting till now had only been 10 minutes.

A cold claw clamped its fingers around her heart. She knew that her husband had been alive ten minutes ago, but was he still alive now? "Mom," Candice said from the back, "I think Robert's been shot."

"What, damn, damn! Damn!" She stopped the vehicle, got out and looked at the right passenger door and realized that there were three bullet holes in it. One must have found its way into her son. She popped the door and Robert groaned and leaned forward, his head going into the driver's head rest. Her heart sank as she saw the red spot in his side. She leaned him over, back onto Candice's side. Her reasoning was that she did not want to pull him out and then have to tend to him on the side of the road. That would have made them exposed and unable to run if they were suddenly attacked. She rolled him over onto his side and checked the wound. Ripping his shirt, she saw where the bullet went in, and to her dismay she realized that there was no exit wound which meant that she would have to try and locate it.

She understood that there was no way she could do it here; she would have to really get to their bug out location and go into doctor mode. There was no time to lose. She felt his pulse. It was still strong, although he was semi-conscious. "Candice you will have to hold this cloth over the wound. Talk to him, keep him awake. When we get to the camp we will get that bullet out of him." She looked at her daughter half expecting to hear cries of panic but instead her daughter calmly placed her hand over the improvised bandage. Her eyes were clear and had a hardness to them that almost broke Samantha's heart. It amazed Sam just how quickly the young adapted. Candice shook her head in the affirmative, and her mom slammed the door, got back in, and gunned the engine. The Tahoe bucked and then they were off again. Samantha was not thinking about her husband then. It was all about getting to the camp and saving her son's life.
*

They pulled into the camp thirty minutes later. She got out and unhooked the barbed wire gate, then pulled the car in. She drove into the little sheltered area they had made to hide the car from the road.

Robert was drifting out of consciousness again. They got him to come around and he moaned in pain as they dragged him out and began the quarter mile hike to the cabin. It was the hardest thing Candice had ever done but she resolved to keep her mouth shut and deal with it. She had sat silently the last two years, and especially the last six months, and had watched as her parents worried themselves silly about everything. She knew that they did not want them to be too exposed to the reality of what was going on. But that was impossible. It was impossible because she knew fundamentally that life was changed when she had stopped going to school.

No matter how serious things got, school was always in session. It was one of the standards of normalcy. There were always natural disasters in the US. A tornado could come through and destroy a town, destroy the schools. She knew that usually within two weeks things would be back to normal. They would find a shack somewhere if it came to that, and school would get going again. Then there would be some TV news story of the folks getting their lives back on track. Well there was no school for the past 6 months. So yes she knew that despite her parents trying to shield them from the worst of it, there was no denying that life as she had known it was a thing of the past. That pre-collapse world was gone for good most likely. Her and her brother's world would now be very different.

Candice knew that this was her chance to do her part; she was not a stupid shallow child. Her parents had raised her a lot better than that. Her job now was to help carry her brother's almost dead weight of 155 lbs all the way to the cabin and help her mother save his life. It all came down to this; she realized then very clearly that she would do anything to preserve the small circle of people who were her family. That's why she didn't like it that her father had decided they had to split up.

She was absolutely terrified when she heard the conversation between her parents earlier. She wondered if Dad was still alive. She gritted her teeth, and holding Robert under the shoulders she half trotted with her mom up the small track to the cabin. "Almost there." She heard her mother say. They grunted and ran, walked in short quick bursts. Shortly they came upon the absolutely beautiful sight of the cabin up ahead. Then she heard her mother curse. She lifted her head and saw why her mother was mad. The cabin door was open and two people came out and stood still, watching them intently. Her mom came to a rigid stop and swore again softly. This was something not expected. Robert moaned and that spurred her forward. As she got closer she realized that she recognized the people who were standing there. They were the Pywoskis. The man was wearing blue jeans and dirty heavy jacket, and he looked like he hadn't shaved in a really long time. The woman was dirty, with stringy brown hair and was dressed in jeans like her husband and wore a heavy black sweater. They had their hands in their pockets as the party came up into the small clearing in the yard. They made no moves to help and just stepped aside as Samantha went into the cabin.

Samantha laid her son out on the floor and immediately went to work. She gave orders to Candice who responded automatically. They got hot water going. She went down into the root cellar and brought out the emergency medical kit. She cleared a space around her son, making sure there was enough light, took what was left of his shirt off and did a preliminary inspection of the wound. Her breath caught in her throat as she realized that it was very bad. His stomach was swollen and tender. Even more troubling was that the bullet had not exited, which meant that she would have to get in there and find it. There was nothing worse than a shifting piece of lead inside the body.

"Okay, Candice I'm going to have to go in after it. I think I know where it is but if I am wrong this could get a whole lot worse really fast. Your job is to shine the light on the incision. If you feel sick then just put it down and make sure that I can still see because I cannot afford to make a mistake here." She looked at her daughter and saw that she was as white as a sheet, her eyes strangely shiny. She also became aware of the other people crowding in and closing the door. She had forgotten about just how cold it really was. She took a deep breath and began to work. All her training and experience as an RN was going to be tested now.

She gave Robert a shot of morphine, enough to deaden the pain as well as knock him out. The last thing she wanted was to have him moving around while she was trying to locate the bullet. Normally for a wound like this, the first thing that would have been done was to wheel him into X-Ray. Locating the bullets fragments and stopping any internal bleeding would have been top priority. In a flash she realized just how desperately dangerous this all was. It brought home that they were now on a very 19th century level of existence. She shook her head and got started.
*

Alfred wondered if his family had made it to the cabin. He figured he had given them a good chance and that had to do it for now. He shook his head trying not to think too much about it; his job was to stay alive tonight. It had been a fairly mild winter in upstate New York so far, but he knew that tonight the temperature would probably dip into the low 30's. This was like some weird TV reality survival dilemma show. Only there weren't any cameras around and there was no crew on standby in case he ran into serious trouble. He was on his own and he knew that getting through the coming night was going to be a very difficult task.

He assessed himself as he limped along. He had no matches, nor would he wish to start a fire that would give away his location to anyone out there. He had on his Parka which had kept him fairly warm when he was moving, but he knew that as soon as he became stationary and the temperature dropped to near or below freezing, he would begin to freeze. He also knew that his injury was the X factor in all of this as well. How his body responded to the wound over the next couple of hours would be the key to his survival. If the wound became infected and he became sick and delirious, he would die for sure.

He looked at the sky, and his watch. It was already 4 o'clock. He knew that in another hour he would lose all the light. So he began to look around for a likely place to make camp. He came to a thick stand of trees and when he looked in, he realized that it had a nice little hidden dip that was perfect for just crawling in and bedding down until first light. The ground in the little enclosure was already deeply covered in leaves, so he began dragging some fallen pine branches into the small enclosure. He dug down and shoved the branches under the leaves, creating a little pocket that he could slip into. His plan was to crawl into his leafy hole, cover himself as completely as he could and sleep.

The leaves had collected in a nice mound a few feet deep between the overshadowing trees. He realized that he was lucky that they were dry

underneath. He decided not to waste any more daylight. He dug himself in and covered himself up. Then slowly he began to get warm. It was working. He felt a grateful feeling of exultation. Soon he began to get drowsy and in under an hour he was asleep.
*

There were screams, hazy indistinct sounds finding their way into his consciousness. At first he thought he was dreaming, and there was a moment of confusion as he fought the urge to scream and shake the leaves off himself. Something in his mind made him remain still as his brain fought for control of itself. His breathing began to slow and he realized where he was. Buried, yes that's it; he had buried himself under a couple feet of leaves to keep warm. It was creepy waking up covered that way, and he once again suppressed the urge to shake off the lifesaving natural cover. Something was wrong. He had to find out what it was. Very slowly and carefully he made a hole so he could see into the surrounding woods, and what he saw made his stomach turn to ice.

It was very dark but a group of people were in the clearing to his left. They had made a camp fire and a bigger fire in a pit that they had dug. He could make out at least four women and about ten or nine men. They were all horribly dirty and haggard looking, and on closer inspection he realized why they made the hairs on the back of his neck stand up. He realized that they were all a bit crazy. It was amazing that he was able to recognize this just from the way they moved and interacted. There was a horrid look of desolation and wildness about them that made him involuntarily slow his breathing and dig himself further into the hole while he kept an eye on them.

He knew that 'The Collapse' had been tough on people, but here he was witnessing first-hand the desperation it had driven some to. He wondered if they were a family or just random people. There were no children in the group. The women had set about tending the fire, stoking it up. They obviously felt that their numbers made them big enough to take care of any threats. They hammered a pole at each end of the pit, and the fact that they were going to obviously cook a meal made Alfred's stomach do a loop. He began to salivate.

He could now feel the heat from the fire. Whatever they were going to cook must be a huge animal, he realized by the size of the pit. There was a commotion, and the men dragged in a middle aged man. He was wearing a ripped up dirty white shirt, grey pants and dress shoes that had begun to fall apart. He was badly beaten and bleeding, and his captors rained blows down on him, forcing him to move forward. Alfred felt his breath catch in his throat as he realized what they were about to do. They forced the victim down on his stomach. They used some chains to tie him to a pole, which Alfred realized was the spit that they were going to use to roast him. The man sobbed and then he began to beg, asking them to kill him. An insane man with pale scraggly long shoulder length hair took a long sharp knife from a sheath at his waist, went over to the man and cut his throat.

Alfred would never forget the sound of a man dying because his throat had been cut. He had read many books and seen many horror films but the awful sucking-choking sounds the victim made as his blood pumped out into the ground made Alfred break out in a sweat despite the cold. He realized that he was never as scared in his life as he was then. He watched as the skinny man ran the knife over a whet stone before cutting off the man's head and tossing it like a ball into the pit. There were sparks as the head and blood hit the coals and the flesh began to sizzle at once. The man then dressed the body, just like how one would field dress an animal. He cut the clothes off, and then he cut the body open from the sternum to the groin, taking the intestines out. He removed the internal organs, throwing choice bits on the fire to roast.

When he was done the other men hoisted the body up and placed it across the fire to cook. The smell of the roasting man filled the air, and much to his revolution it made Alfred's mouth water. It smelled like roasting pork. Then he became violently nauseous, and sick of himself. He felt horrified that his own body would react the way it did. What these people were doing was an abomination. He understood what it meant to be cold and hungry and desperate, but he would never do this. He would put a bullet in himself first, and he knew that on an elemental level.

This went on for about an hour before they began cutting off parts of the body with knives. The men ate first then the women had their share. Then one of the men, a man of medium height and build with a face so dirty it appeared as if he wore a mask, reached into the fire and fished out the sizzling head. It would have been easy for Alfred to slip back into his cover of leaves and not watch anymore, but he ground his teeth and forced himself to watch.

 The men actually kicked the head around. It rolled among them sounding like a fleshy gourd. There was laughter now among the group and they chatted and joked about this and that. Their bellies were full, Alfred noted with horrid fascination, and they were now relaxed. Another man began passing around a large aluminum can from which they all drank. One woman picked up the head and using her fingers she reached down into the eye socket and scooped out the jellied eyeball. She popped it into her mouth and licked her lips with relish. One of the other women beckoned for the now cooled head and she rolled it to her. She then proceeded to do the same to the other eye.

They then took the remaining meat from the spit to prevent it from burning and quickly cut the rest of it into strips, rubbing something on it that looked like salt, next placing it into a large canvas bag. One of the men took one of the women away from the clearing to a secluded spot, and they could be heard copulating. Soon all the women and men went off to their own spot together. This went on for about an hour before Alfred realized that it was suddenly all quiet. Sounds of snores could be heard as the fires slowly died down.

Alfred didn't think that he could sleep after what he had just witnessed, and as a matter of fact he thought that he should stay awake just in case they discovered his hiding place. He tried, but he could not hold on to consciousness. It had been a long day and an even longer night. He soon surrendered to his exhaustion.
*

When he woke in the morning it was to the sounds of the *cannibal gang*— that was just what he called them—going about their morning chores. He really started to hope that they would break camp soon because he needed to get going. He quietly checked himself out. Physically he felt about the same as he did the evening after he had been shot. He was not running a fever, which would have been disastrous. That would have been a sign that his wound was most likely infected. The place where he had been injured throbbed, but he figured that was normal. He would have to change the bandage as soon as he could. He would eat a bit more of the yellow root as well as put some on the wound, it seemed to be working. His head was clear. He quickly checked his firearm. He had two full clips left, and he had 7 rounds in the pistol. There were nine of the cannibal gang, and he did not want to fight them. So he resolved to wait it out.

After about 10 AM he realized that they were going to go out on a 'raid' as they called it. The guy with the thinning long hair, who had butchered the body last night, gave the instructions, and it seemed that they would leave three people in the camp and the rest would go on the raid. After the main body of the gang had left the clearing and were gone for what Alfi estimated was long enough to be out of hearing, just in case he had to use his gun, he decided to make his move. Very quietly he emerged from his hiding place and while the three camp guards were doing their work around the camp, he slipped out of the clearing. As he moved he realized that his right leg was indeed a little tight and sore. He hoped that it would improve with movement.

Just as he thought that he was in the clear, he came face to face with one of the gang who had gone out to look for wood and had circled back in a wide arc; the woman was a pale emaciated brunette, who smelled like bad cheese. She dropped her pile of wood and screamed. Alfred did not hesitate. The .45 banged once and the female cannibal went down in a heap. His heart lurched in his chest as he tried to move forward as quickly as he could. All his senses seemed to come on line all at once. The shot had alerted the men who were back at the camp, and he could hear them coming towards him. He could not outrun them that much he knew, so it was a stand and fight scenario. He hoped none of them had guns.

He decided that he had to get the odds in his favor. He looked around his surroundings quickly and decided on a plan of action. It was also then he decided that if he survived this encounter and made it to camp, he would always wear camouflage, or clothes with which he could better blend into his environment. He actually ran towards the sounds of the pursuit and then made sure that he picked a spot were the men would see the body in the clearing. He hoped that the shock of coming upon the body of their dead counterpart would give him enough time to bring them down.

He crouched in a shallow defile and waited. He hoped that the men would run by and into the clearing where the body lay. Then he could basically shoot them while they were distracted. Some people would have met the men face to face. They would have been bothered by the whole not shooting a man in the back thing. As far as Alfred was concerned, all he cared about was keeping the odds in his favor so that he could see his family again. He had no intention of direct confrontation if he could help it. He heard the men running through the brush, and ducked as they went by. They came to a dead stop about thirty feet past him. They had reached the clearing and had just seen the body. He did not wait for them to fully understand and get organized. He got himself into a kneeling firing position. He squeezed the trigger, and one man dropped and the other went down as he was turning towards his partner.

Alfred ran forward as quickly as his injured leg allowed. One man was still moving. He shot him again and all movements ceased. He then decided to get as far and as fast away from there as he could. He wondered if his family was safe.

*

Samantha had located the bullet. She had followed the entry wound as carefully as she could, probing until she located the piece of lead and pulled it out with a pair of tweezers. There was something that caused her a lot of concern; it had lodged itself next to Robert's spine. In some ways she would have preferred the bullet to have passed clean through his body, but not the spine of course. She did not know how much damage it had done to the spine and all they could do now was hope for the best. She cleaned herself up and made Robert as comfortable as she could.

Then she turned her attention to the Pywoskis. It was already very late in the evening and she wondered where her husband was and if she would ever see him again. All she wanted to do was to crawl into bed, but she now had to find out what her two friends in another life were doing here. They were outside and were sitting on the two small steps that led to the cabin. She really looked at them and was surprised to see how thin and tired and beaten they appeared. Janice must have lost thirty pounds and Peter even more. He looked so thin it seemed like he would tip over if the wind caught his frail body. It was their eyes that really got her attention. They seemed glassy and a bit crazy. "How long have you been here?"

"Ohhh, about a week. We had to leave our home. Peter would go looking for food while I watched the house. One day a group of people came and ran us off. They took everything of value that we had, and basically took over our neighborhood. We were on the streets for a while, trying to find food and staying away from all the gangs. I really thought we were going to die. Then Peter remembered that you had bought this piece of land up here. We decided to check it out. When we came at first we did not find anything. We thought that you did not have time to develop the place. Then Peter found the trail and it led us to the house and the food." She started to cry then. It was a low mournful sobbing. "This place saved our lives, now we will have to leave it. You guys saw all of this coming didn't you."

"We had a feeling something was going to happen. Alfred just decided that it was good to be ready in case there was a problem, I am glad he acted on his instincts."

"You guys really did a good job getting this place ready. All we found was the food in the cabinets, but I am sure you got it outfitted to last awhile. If Alfred is anything the man is thorough." Peter took his glasses off, it made him look even smaller and more vulnerable. The mischievous smile and optimism of the past was gone.

"What about your family?" Samantha asked.

"Well Mom and Dad live in a little village outside of Seattle, and the last time I heard anything from them was five months ago when the cell towers were still working. I don't know if they are even alive." Peter smiled wryly and put his glasses back on.

"Well my Mom is still alive, or was alive," Janice sighed. It was a desperate, dry rattling sound.

"She was in that home, you remember because she had a bad stroke. I don't know if she is okay or not." Samantha quietly surmised that the answer was not. No one would have the resources to keep those homes going. Chances were that all the vulnerable people who needed others to care for them were abandoned soon after things went south. It was horrible to contemplate the fate of all those people who were bedridden, or suffered from some debilitating disease or physical infirmity and needed someone to keep them alive. 'The death toll from this when it's all over is going to be in the hundreds of millions or more,' she thought grimly.

She looked at the growing moon and wondered if her husband was still alive. It was then she said, "When Alfred gets here we'll have a chat about the two of you staying on. I won't guarantee anything but we will see what we can do."

Janice smiled wanly and grabbed Peter's hand; he squeezed her hand in return. They sat on the steps for a while before going in. Samantha decided for just one night to relax the routine they had established at the first house, which was always to have someone on watch. She figured that no one knew that the cabin was there so maybe they could just sleep through the night, just getting up to check on Robert. He was breathing easily and would most likely sleep through the next few hours, and that, Samantha thought, would be good. She made her bed on the floor next to Robert's bunk. Candice would share the larger front room with her, while the Pywoskis would stay in the smaller room in the back.

While she fixed her makeshift bed roll beside the bed of her wounded son, she thought about her daughter Candice. The kid had handled herself really well while she performed the surgery on Robert. There was a small glow of pride in her when she thought of the way her daughter had very calmly assisted, and there had been no sign of panic even when she had to make the incision to recover the bullet. Candice's calm had steadied her own nerves. Her daughter had shown a lot of grit today. Both her children had during the crisis shown that they were able to think and function under a lot of pressure.

Once again she reflected on the long term effects all these horrible experiences would have, not only on the children but on her and Alfred as well. The thought of her husband brought an involuntary gasp and she crawled into the sleeping bag, her hands tightened into little fists of tension. As she turned over onto her back she realized that she had not taken her .38 pistol from her waist holster. She decided that she would just let it remain where it was and call it a night. Her last conscious thoughts before slipping into sleep were about her husband. She remembered a time when they made love on their back deck.

*

Candice tried breathing but couldn't. At first in her dream she was swimming on some beach. She went under the water but could not seem to come up for air. She was struggling, fighting, but she couldn't get her head above water. She gathered her strength and made one last gasp and push for the surface. Her head came up and, blink, blink. The dream world blended with reality and then she was awake and choking. Someone was on top of her. The person was heavy and straddling her chest. She tried screaming out but only a choked cry escaped her. Someone's fingers were around her throat, and then a fist slammed into her face. The pain was brutal and overwhelming. Reality swam away for an instant and came back. The room was dark and the struggle had a nightmarish edge to it.

She saw stars and when her head cleared she realized that the fingers were back around her throat. She also knew then that the person was trying to kill her. 'This is what it feels like to have someone wanting you gone. You were no longer a person to them, just an obstacle that had to be removed.' Something then occurred, she realized that she would only have a few minutes left to live if she did not act, and act decisively. She curled her feet which were wrapped in the heavy blanket and pushed her herself backward. It was enough, because her head slammed into the wall behind her. Her assailant was tipped forward and thudded into the wall as well. Candice got her hands free and began punching. Her fist connected with a chest and then she struck out again, and this time she connected with lips and teeth. The person cried out and tried to grab her again. Candice reached out to where she knew she had placed a flashlight. She grabbed the little light and switched it on. The beam caught something that made her blood run cold and she screamed, "Moooommm!"
*

Samantha had to get up to check on Robert. The alarm on her watch vibrated. She had set it for every other hour. Candice would check on him in between and in this way he would be monitored throughout the night. There was really nothing else she could do for her son now. He would sleep through the night and when he awoke his condition would be clearer. She was always a light sleeper anyway, and just before the alarm went off she thought she heard Candice mumble something. As she laid on her side looking at the stars in the sky over Robert's bunk, she listened to him breathing faintly, and thought for the thousandth time just what a horrible couple of days they had endured as a family.

She heard Candice moan again and thought that her daughter must be having an intense dream. She felt deeply sad at this thought. They all would be having bad dreams and nightmares for awhile. She was about to get up when she heard a shuffling movement and she thought that perhaps Candice just could not sleep and had gotten out of bed. She turned in the direction of the sound and then saw something that took her breath away.

There was a thump, a cry and then another cry of pain. Then a light shone out. It was Candice's flashlight. What she did next saved her life. She saw a pair of jeans a few feet away from her, they came towards her, and she moved to boost herself up on Robert's bed. Just then an axe buried itself where her head had just been. She heard Candice scream, "Mom!" Someone attacked Candice and the flashlight went flying leaving her in the deep semi darkness again. She pulled the .38 from the holster and fired at the silhouette in from of her. The person went backwards with a cry of surprise. She fired again and the figure crumpled. She could still hear her daughter and the other individual struggling. It sounded desperate as furniture was now being overturned and glass could be heard breaking.

She got a hold of her flashlight, held it under her pistol and shone the light on the struggling pair. Candice was on the bottom, her friend Janice was on top. Janice's face was contorted into a furious mask of rage. In her hand she had a piece of wood that was going to be used for the stove. "Janice! Don't!" The woman let out a blood curdling scream as she raised the firewood over her head. Samantha squeezed the trigger again. Her shot was true; it hit Janice under her arm in the right side. She collapsed on top of Candice who screamed and pushed her off. She moaned and moved a few times then was still.

Samantha's legs felt like jelly and suddenly she wanted to vomit badly. She ran for the door and emptied the contents of her stomach into the bushes outside the cabin. She began to cry, and then stopped herself. She shoved the pistol back into the holster, and went back inside the cabin. Her daughter threw herself into her arms; she buried her head in her chest and cried. She held Candice and let her cry herself out. Then they gingerly began moving about the cabin. Samantha found an oil lamp and lit it. The scene it revealed was grizzly and unsettling in the flickering light cast by the flame.

Peter was lying face up; his eyes were open in death. There was blood pooling from his throat and there was a big red hole in the middle of his chest where he had been shot. Both women got him by the feet and dragged him out to the front of the house. They then got Janice who had collapsed on her side and died, and dragged her out beside her husband. Samantha did not have the mental energy to do any more tonight. She checked once more on her son, sat down beside his bunk on the ground and hugged her daughter. There would be no more thought of getting any sleep tonight.
*

Chapter Eight: Flames

Alfred limped his way along. He stayed off the main roads, and finally he reached what he knew was the dairy farm that bordered his own land. He could have stuck to the woods, but he decided just to see how his closest neighbor had fared. He gingerly climbed over the fence. The .45 was in his shoulder holster under his jacket. He wanted to have his hands free just in case someone spotted him. Maybe they would think he was non-hostile. He had another four bullets left in the magazine; he hoped he didn't have to use them.

The day was a typical wintry day for upstate New York. Cold and grey, the dark cloudy skies signaled the possibility of snow later on in the day. He counted himself lucky so far that the weather and temperature had been good since the separation from his family. He made his way from what he knew was an outlying field towards the cow barns he had usually seen from the road during his drives to and from the bug out cabin. He stopped cold as the sight before him tightened his stomach into what he now recognized as his body going on red alert.

The large barn had been burned. He looked into the destroyed structure and saw the remains of people inside. From where he stood he counted eight skulls. The bones were all huddled together at what must have been a large barred window. He surmised that they must have been herded into the barn and then it was set alight. He did not see any animal bones in the carnage. That pointed to the fact that raiders must have taken the cows as well as any other food from the farm before moving on. This pointed to a rather large group that was out there.

He stuck his hands in his pockets and kept moving. He walked past the farmhouse that had also been burnt. He then came across a sight that made him stop. A low hiss escaped from his teeth. In the grass near the house there were the skeleton remains of a young baby. He did not know then why this bothered him the way it did. But he found that he was rooted to the spot, and after a while he found a piece of board which he used to dig a shallow grave. He buried the baby, and as he patted the earth onto the bones he sat down heavily and sobbed. His body went limp and he cried. Great heaving sobs came from his throat and he did not realize that he had curled into a ball, groaning and choking back the sobs that felt as if they would tear his body apart.

He had seen a lot of awful things since 'The Collapse', but there was something in this that brought home the awful truth of the extent of the calamity that had befallen the globe. Once again he felt bitterness towards the people who had let everything get so out of hand. Those people who should have kept the well-being of the citizens and country at the top of their priorities but were bought off, they had gotten caught up in their own petty quarrels and machinations while the country had disintegrated. He felt a sore loss for his country. The USA was the beacon of light to so many. Its unique Constitution should have inspired the world. He wondered if one day its citizens would be able to rebuild the country and how long it would take.

He did not know how long he laid there, in some kind of stupor over the bones of a child he did not know, but in a very tragic way did. He got up brushed himself off and left the farm behind. He had been a survivor of 'The Collapse' now for almost five months. He marveled how much the country had disintegrated in the 150 days or so since the economic system crashed. How could it all have gone so bad so fast? How could no one bring any kind of order?

As he walked through the woods on his way to his family's bug out camp, he understood that the last twenty three hours had taught him the most fundamental lessons that he would have to internalize to give his family a chance of making it through to the other side. What would the new world look like he wondered?

He was now in very familiar surroundings. He knew the features of his land well. He was just a few minutes from home. He decided to be cautious and he began to tread a little more carefully. He became completely switched on. As he neared the cabin he saw something that made him gasp. There were two bodies covered with a sheet outside the cabin door. He crouched in the bushes and waited, viciously suppressing the urge to run at the cabin screaming his head off. He looked down and noticed that the .45 was in his hand. He did not remember drawing it from the holster. He heard noises inside the cabin; he waited to see who would emerge. It was agony as his eyes went repeatedly to the corpses under the sheet. Then a woman emerged and he stifled a cry of joy as he waited until the other female emerged, they were safe. He walked out of the woods to his family.
*

They buried the bodies of their one time friends as far away from the cabin as they thought necessary and safe. They remembered the countless times they had

had dinner with Peter and Janice Pywoski. The trips they all took together, the laughs they had, had with their friends. The Aimeses held each other close, in the woods. The reality of a world where one's best friends would kill you for food and shelter made it clear that the only people they could really trust were each other.

Samantha was feeling a bit optimistic because Robert had woken up, and although it was early he seemed like he would make it. The one caveat was that he could not move his legs. One hurdle at a time she thought. She had also patched up her husband and was amazed that it seemed that the yellow root had kept his wound from getting infected. She resolved to keep her eyes open for it when she went out into the woods. She also resolved to teach Candice everything she knew about medicine; they would all have to become learners now. It would take a lot more know-how to survive in this post Collapse world.

They took a close look at their supplies and realized that the Pywoskis had only found the food in the cabin's cabinets. They had not discovered the massive root cellar or the keys to the containers. Most of their food supplies were still intact. There were still a lot of preparations to make this homestead more secure, and they went about the work with a grim determination.

On the second evening Alfred got the ham radio out and tuned the dial to the lower bands, found that Donald Rovey was somehow miraculously still on the air. Both he and Samantha looked at each other and held hands as they listened to the old journalist. Candice spooned hot soup into Robert as the old man gave his report.

"Hi folks this is Donald Rovey coming to you from an undisclosed location. Some friends of mine, a good buddy Jasper, came and got me out of the old radio station and now we are somewhere with a group of people who are intent on keeping themselves alive and hidden until this all comes to an end. Let me bring you all up to date on what my little birds have been telling me."

"Well don't trust the army; anyone in a green uniform is not a friend. The military has been rounding up civilians and taking them to labor camps. That's right folks, they have begun gathering whatever they can use and forcing the civilians to work in factories or grow food. Doesn't sound so bad when I say it, or when you hear it, but from what I have been told those camps are a living hell. Most people don't get out of them.

"It has been told to me that some of the military personnel did leave to be with their families and most left when they realized that they were no longer protecting American citizens or really the State. They were in actuality protecting and carrying out the orders of a government that had betrayed its people. A government that was no longer legitimate."

"There have been riots all over America and most governmental leaders are in hiding. It has come out that most were in the pocket of the big banks and big corporations that drove the country to its knees. Massive incompetence and greed caused this calamity. The question I ask you my dear listeners is how do we get things back together again? From what I have heard certain survival groups as well as rogue military groups are making claims for the leadership of country. If you can, stay away from these groups also. They claim that they are making and are keeping order, but they *are just people who are now seizing the opportunity to control their own territories."*

"From what I have heard of the rest of the world, it is bad all over and it is especially bad in Europe. From my fellow hams I have been told that there has been a total disintegration of the European countries as we know it. As one person said, it has gone positively medieval. The world, my dear listeners, is in flames. Well that's all I have for tonight I will be with you again God's willing same time tomorrow. Goodnight."

Alfred turned off the radio and looked at his family. Five months in and they were all still here. He knew that for them to survive the coming storm they would have to plan and prepare, for anything that could go wrong, would. This bug out location was just a respite from the challenges that were to come. He wondered if they could survive it.
*

Dear readers there will be more to come.
The End, for now...

5603657R00072

Made in the USA
San Bernardino, CA
14 November 2013